Dear Reader,

Home, family, community and love. These are the values we cherish most in our lives—the ideals that ground us, comfort us, move us. They certainly provide the perfect inspiration around which to build a romance collection that will touch the heart.

And so we are thrilled to offer you the Harlequin Heartwarming series. Each of these special stories is a wholesome, heartfelt romance imbued with the traditional values so important to you. They are books you can share proudly with friends and family. And the authors featured in this collection are some of the most talented storytellers writing today, including favorites such as Roz Denny Fox, Amy Knupp and Mary Anne Wilson. We've selected these stories especially for you based on their overriding qualities of emotion and tenderness, and they center around your favorite themes—children, weddings, second chances, the reunion of families, the quest to find a true home and, of course, sweet romance.

So curl up in your favorite chair, relax and prepare for a heartwarming reading experience!

Sincerely,

The Editors

AMY KNUPP

Amy Knupp lives in Wisconsin with her husband, two sons, five cats and a turtle named Scuttle. She graduated from the University of Kansas with degrees in French and journalism and feels lucky to use very little of either one in her writing career. She's a member of Novelists, Inc., Romance Writers of America, Mad City Romance Writers and Wisconsin Romance Writers. In her spare time she enjoys reading, college basketball and addictive computer games. To learn more about Amy and her stories, visit www.amyknupp.com.

HARLEQUIN HEARTWARMING

Amy Knupp

Return to Lone Oak

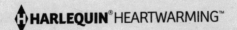

Recycling programs
for this product may
not exist in your area.

ISBN-13: 978-0-373-36621-7

RETURN TO LONE OAK

Copyright © 2013 by Amy Knupp

Originally published as DOCTOR IN HER HOUSE
Copyright © 2007 by Amy Knupp

HARLEQUIN®
™ www.Harlequin.com

Printed in U.S.A.

Return to Lone Oak

To Camden and Colton...
two of the very best cheerleaders anyone
could ever ask for. I love you guys!
To Justin...once again, and even more so
than usual, I couldn't have done this without
your support and understanding
(and repeated talking down from the ledge).
I'm incredibly lucky to have you.

CHAPTER ONE

KATIE SALINGER SWALLOWED her annoyance at being injured and pasted a smile on her face as the door opened. She thought the world of old Dr. Fletcher.

Except it wasn't old Dr. Fletcher who walked into the examining room.

"Hello, Katie," the tall thirtysomething man said, scanning her chart.

"Where's Dr. Fletcher?"

"That's me. Noah Fletcher."

She stared at him blankly.

"I'm Ivan Fletcher's son."

The light dawned. Katie remembered years ago seeing family photos in Dr. Fletcher's offices. One kid, a son. At least ten years older than she was. Katie had never known his name. Never cared. But that was long before she'd found herself stuck in a small room with the man—with a gaping wound in need of stitches.

Okay, *more* stitches.

"You're the baseball player." He'd been wearing his uniform in several of those pictures, she now recalled.

He made eye contact. "A long time ago. High school." His eyes were green with flecks of gold. He returned his attention to the notes on Katie's chart.

"Looks like you have some kind of death wish," he said with an arch of his eyebrow. "Rollerblading with previous injuries?"

"Cars kill a lot more people than Rollerblades."

"Not in Lone Oak, Kansas."

"You have a lot of Rollerblade deaths here?" she asked, pushing a strand of hair off her face. "Wouldn't surprise me, actually, with the condition of the sidewalks."

She rarely wiped out on her skates unless she was trying to learn a new trick, but some of the uneven walkways in this town were like minefields for a skater.

And the streets… The ones that weren't paved in hundred-year-old brick had more craters than the moon.

Dr. Fletcher looked as if he were about to debate further. His chest expanded as he drew a deep breath. Causing others to need deep, patience-gathering breaths was something Katie excelled in.

"You injured yourself three days ago doing…what?" he asked.

"Kayaking in Colorado. Ever been?"

He absently shook his head, while continuing to grill her. "You have a broken wrist and you *had*…" he paused to consult her chart again "…twelve stitches in your chin. Rollerblading doesn't seem like the best idea to me."

"Good exercise. I wore pads. A helmet."

"My point is, now you need me to redo your stitches."

"Yes."

"How do I know this won't be a weekly occurrence?"

"Think of me as easy money." She smiled and tapped her foot on the rubber-covered surface of the table. "Could we get this over with? Please?"

Instead of jumping to grant her wish, the doctor continued to flip through her medical file. "You understand my signature is required by your employers before you can return to work?"

"I was hoping Dr. Fletcher could handle it."

"I *am* Dr. Fletcher."

This guy had the humor of a rattlesnake.

"Will getting your approval be a problem?"

"Only if I see you in here again with a new injury. Take care of yourself, heal and I'll be happy to sign. No more of the daredevil activities."

She frowned, her shoulders sagging. "Is Rollerblading considered 'daredevil'?"

He looked her squarely in the eyes. "Give it a couple weeks, at least."

"What about jogging?"

"Can you run without popping your stitches again?"

"I'll do my best."

Jogging bored her to tears, but it'd get her out and about. Keep her active and in shape. She loved being back in her family's old, familiar home, but she wasn't one to sit still for long, no matter where she was.

"Try to take it easy, for your own sake. Let your body rest. You're young, but you still need plenty of healing time." Dr. Fletcher closed her file and rose from his stool. She braced herself. Placing one of his hands on her cheek, he gently rubbed a pungent-smelling disinfectant on her chin. Which stung like crazy, in spite of his tender touch.

"I'm going to deaden the area now."

"You're very kind."

He was about to swab her face a second time but stopped, his hand in midair, and stared at her thoughtfully. She smiled, but his green eyes were shielded, giving away nothing.

"Isn't a nurse supposed to prep me?" Katie asked.

"I'm a hands-on kind of guy."

Otherwise known as a control freak, she'd guess.

He rubbed the numbing agent on her skin, then came at her with an injection of local anesthetic to finish the job.

"Normally people like to close their eyes for this," he said patiently.

"I'm not often accused of being normal."

"Somehow, I'm not surprised."

She was silent as he gave her the shot and explained they would need to wait fifteen minutes for it to take effect. Katie nodded, checking her watch.

"Of course, you're familiar with the whole procedure."

"Yes, sir. And for the record, you've done a much better job so far than they did in Colorado."

He met her gaze and his features relaxed a little. If he wasn't a doctor, she might even entertain the thought that he was good-looking, with his collar-length brown hair and his stubborn jaw. Oh, okay, he *was* nice to look at, but she was a far cry from interested.

Cleary, he was stuffy. Older than her twenty-six years. More serious than a gaggle of nuns. The kind of guy who would rather organize his sock drawer than be social. Definitely not her type.

Dr. Fletcher left, and she listened to his footsteps fading down the hallway. This nondescript room could make a girl climb its bland walls. A pastel print on the faded wallpaper, an antiseptic odor hanging in the air and not a single window. The decor hadn't changed since she'd been a kid. No way could she sit here for the fifteen minutes he'd said it would take for the numbness to kick in.

Katie opened the door and walked into the narrow beige-carpeted hallway. In her socks, she wound her way toward the reception area to look for a magazine. Dr. Fletcher of the younger variety might be a stranger to her, but Katie knew this place of his intimately. She'd been here far more than her share when she was growing up.

Medical clinics were a fact of life for girls who learned to climb trees and scale walls by the age of three. In fact, the elder Dr. Fletcher had regularly joked about naming one of the exam rooms after her.

The young Dr. F, however, didn't seem quite so amused by her frequent-flier status. His problem. He didn't *need* to be amused, as long as he signed off on her health forms. Without his signature, her editor wouldn't let her go back to work. *Company policy.* She'd have to make a point of not winding up here again during the six weeks she was off work, other than for routine checks on her wrist and chin, and the hip she'd bruised.

She headed to the magazine rack, scanning the neat stacks for *her* magazine, but she wasn't surprised when she didn't see it among the *People*s, *Life*s and *Field & Stream*s.

"So you're Katie Salinger."

Katie couldn't tell if the woman speaking to her thought that was a good thing or a bad thing. She looked toward the receptionist's desk. A petite dark-haired woman about Katie's age stared back at her with interested eyes.

"Yeah. Am I in trouble?" Katie asked, as she approached the counter.

"I've read your articles." The woman did a quick check over her shoulder and then stood. "I'm Eve Peterson. Jealous fan."

Katie relaxed when Eve smiled. "Nice to meet you. So you read *Rush?*"

"You bet. Shh." She held up a copy of the latest edition of *Rush* from her desk, then buried it again under some files. "I covet your job every day. Not that this one isn't a barrel of laughs, but I just about peed my pants reading your double black diamond snowboarding article. How cool was that?"

"That was one of my favorites, both the doing and the writing."

Katie tried to remember Eve from school. If she'd grown up here, surely they would've run into each other. Or more accurately they would have known everything there was to know about each other. "Did you go to Lone Oak High?"

"Just for a year. I moved in with my great aunt when I was a senior. Class of oh-six."

"I was two years ahead of you, then. So you've lived here ever since?"

"Mostly. I did a brief college stint. Ran out of money, so here I am." The phone rang. "Speaking of here…"

"I need to get back to my cheery room, anyway."

Katie walked away, grinning as she listened to the very official, very phony voice Eve used to answer the phone.

NOAH STEPPED OUT of Exam Room One, where Kathy, the part-time physician's assistant, had asked for a second opinion on a rash. He glanced at his watch and did a double take. It was already after five. He couldn't figure out how his dad had been handling this volume of patients by himself, especially at the age of sixty-three. Was he trying to work himself into a heart attack?

Noah had come home for his own reasons. Specifically, he was looking for peace and quiet, but now that he was here other worries were absorbing his mind. His parents seemed so *old,* so much more vulnerable than he remembered, and he felt compelled to help them out and try to make their lives easier. Just thinking about them now brought the tension out in the back of his neck.

Noah needed to find a way to cut down on his dad's workload without making him feel incompetent. He planned to carry more than half the weight of the practice, just as soon as he got settled in and accustomed himself to everything and everyone in the office.

Being overloaded with patients would be fine. Being busy up to his eyeballs was exactly what he needed. He'd have less time to think that way.

The woman in Room Four should be numb by now. Katie Salinger, the daredevil. Beautiful and reckless. A dangerous combination, as far as he was concerned.

He braced himself for trouble as he rounded the corner toward her room and ran right into it. Into *her*. He caught one of her arms to steady her, and did his best to avoid looking straight into those intense blue eyes.

"Is something wrong?" he asked.

"No. I just don't like small rooms. I've been getting some doctor-approved exercise."

"Jogging?"

"Walking. I assume that's okay?"

Was she giving him a hard time? Everyone here tiptoed around him, but apparently Katie hadn't gotten the message—or maybe she just chose to ignore it.

Interesting. But not for him to worry about.

"How's the chin? Can you feel anything?" He held the door open for her. As she passed him, her light berry scent snuck past his defenses and challenged his general tendency not to notice such personal details. He turned away and increased the distance between them, annoyed with himself.

"It's dead. I think I'm drooling."

He nodded, satisfied, and automatically steadied her as she climbed onto the table. Then he set to work sewing her stitches, finishing quickly.

"Before you go, I think we need to discuss what's allowed in a little more detail." Call him overcautious, but he didn't trust her for a second.

Katie had been ready to leave, but now she sat back again, clearly less than thrilled.

"Kayaking and Rollerblading are out, at least until your stitches are gone. It'd be best if you didn't do either of those things until your wrist heals, as well. Are there any other dangerous activities you like to participate in?"

"I work for a magazine called *Rush,* as in adrenaline. What do you think?"

The mischief in her eyes was alluring—and familiar. So he looked away. "What do you do for them?"

"Whatever they ask. I write a lot of firsthand-experience reports. You know, hang glide off a mountain, then write about what it was like… I also cover extreme sports competitions, but I usually don't get to participate in them."

He could tell she didn't like being just a spectator. In anything. He knew the type well. She had to flirt with danger, taunt death. Just like Leah. The ache in his neck—which never fully disappeared—climbed higher, blossoming into a full-blown headache.

"Last month I went kite-surfing and swam with sharks."

"How was that?" he asked, thinking surely she was certifiable. Possibly even more so than Leah had been.

"The sharks were terrifying. Can't wait to do it again. Surfing? Awesome. Ever try it?"

"I'm afraid not."

He'd had his share of adventure over the past two years as a volunteer for Medical Missions and he wasn't afraid of taking certain risks. Or at least he hadn't been when he started out. But now he'd come back to Lone Oak for a calmer existence, to build a low-key focused life, where setting bones was as exciting as it got. Kitesurfing was not on his to-do list.

"You should give it a try sometime. There's a great spot in south Texas."

"Highly unlikely."

"Your loss." She shrugged and got off the exam table. "Is the lecture over?"

"For now. I'll see you in a week to remove those stitches. If you haven't taken matters into your own hands again before then."

She bent to pick up the Rollerblades in a corner of the room and then it dawned on him that she must have *skated* here to have her stitches repaired. She had a screw loose. She was tall, golden-brown-haired trouble with a scary dose of invincibility.

When she saw him watching her, she looked almost guilty for a flash. "I wasn't going to skate. I got the message."

"I'm just making sure you take it seriously."

"Of course." She stuffed her socks into the skates, along with her knee and elbow pads, then picked up her bright yellow helmet. As she straightened, she met his eyes. "I can tell you're the type to take everything seriously."

She said it as if it were an insult, but Noah didn't defend himself. From what he'd seen, she could use a large measure of serious.

"Nice to meet you," he said, holding out his hand.

She shoved her helmet under the cast encasing her left arm and took his hand, her shake much softer than he expected. Then she smiled, her eyes sparkling with a zest for life that rocked him with a bone-chilling familiarity.

Trouble, he thought again, as he watched her leave.

KATIE MADE HER WAY to the front desk to pay for her visit.

"All better now?" Eve asked.

"I'm fixed."

Eve told her what her co-payment was and Katie pulled out a debit card.

"So what's the story with the new doc?" Katie asked.

"Ah, Dr. Noah." Eve's voice got quieter. "Not bad to look at, is he?"

"If you don't mind the frown lines."

"I know. He doesn't smile a lot. Tortured soul or something. Which is totally hot. I could almost have a crush."

"Why don't you go for it?"

"Besides the fact that he signs my pay-checks?" Eve shook her head. "I'm not into that 'I've got secrets' thing. He'd make me nuts."

"He has secrets?"

Eve looked over her shoulder to make sure no one was within earshot. "He used to volunteer for one of those healthcare missions or something—he was in Africa for a while. Something happened there that he *does not* talk about."

"How do you know?"

"Any time someone mentions his volunteer work, he immediately shuts them down. Stupid me, I asked him once if something awful had happened there to make him so serious. I was half joking."

"Did he answer?"

"Not with words. But the look on his face told me plenty. And he's been even stiffer with me ever since, as if he thinks he's revealed too much."

"So you think something happened in Africa." Katie wasn't sure why this interested her, but she couldn't help wanting to know more. Chalk it up to the journalist in her.

"You guys talking about Dr. Noah?"

Eve rocked back in surprise at the middle-aged woman who'd sidled up next to her.

"Mandy, I swear I'm gonna put a bell around your neck."

Mandy responded with a low smoker's chuckle. "You know the second you start talking all hushed, I'm gonna wander over here to see what kind of juicy stuff you're discussin'." She rested an ample hip on the desk. "So was I right?"

"Who else from Lone Oak has been to Africa?"

"He took a bullet, is what I heard."

"Who'd you hear that from?"

"His dad."

"What else did he say?" Eve asked as she ran Katie's debit card through the machine.

"Very little. I could tell he's worried as all get-out, though."

Intriguing. Seemed as if no one knew much about the mysterious doctor's past.

"Sign this," Eve said, pointing to a form in front of Katie. "That's one story I'd love to hear."

"Yeah, well, lots of luck," Mandy said as another patient walked up behind Katie to settle her bill. "Time for this girl to call it a day." She headed back to the opposite side of the office and retrieved her purse from a cluttered desk.

Katie made the appointment to have her stitches removed, wondering if she might be able to drag out any additional information regarding Noah Fletcher's past on that return visit.

NOSTALGIA SETTLED OVER KATIE as she turned the corner onto the street where she'd grown up. The walk from the doctor's office—which she made barefoot, carrying her skates, just for the sake of the controlling Dr. Fletcher—was nearly the same route she'd taken day after day on the way home from grade school.

She'd turn that corner each day and squint all the way down to her family's home, to see if her mom, who'd arranged her life so that she'd work only while her girls were in school, was sitting on the front steps waiting. More often than not, if the weather was decent, she was there. Sometimes with a book, sometimes without. Always with a welcoming smile for Katie and her two sisters.

The memory gave Katie some measure of comfort, just as being in their family home often did. No matter how much she raced around the country engaging in the stunts and extreme sports that she loved, coming back home always centered her. Reminded her of the good times, when everything had been simple, happy. That comfort was what had brought her to Lone Oak now, when she was forced to take time off to heal.

When she was still four houses away from the Salinger abode, however, her steps froze. A For Sale by Owner sign was posted front and center in the yard.

No. This wasn't for real. They absolutely couldn't sell that house.

She'd known her dad and Mrs. Hale—she couldn't get used to calling her Claudia—had tossed the idea around now that they were married, but they'd apparently forgotten to fill Katie in on their decision. Or they'd avoided doing so because they knew she'd hate it.

She glanced at the quaint front porch again, wishing for the comfort of her mother's image, thinking of the love in her face. But the image escaped her. She couldn't summon it for anything. She gasped for air, squeezing her eyes shut.

The unfamiliar anxiety paralyzed her for a few seconds, until she opened her eyes again and focused on the anger that was burning inside.

Katie headed straight for the offending sign and heaved it out of the ground. Banging the dirt off the poles onto the concrete sidewalk, not caring if she damaged the sign in the process, she dragged it with her to the back door and barged into the house.

"Dad!"

Claudia, her dad's wife and formerly the family's housekeeper, hurried in from the living room. "What is it, honey?"

"This." She pointed to the sign. "No one told me you were putting the house on the market today."

"We've been talking about it for a long time."

"Seems like you're not talking any more."

Wendell Salinger came into the kitchen

then, carrying his reading glasses. "What's going on, Katie? Why'd you pull the sign up?"

"Don't you think you should tell me about these things first? Talk to me?" She stood the sign against the wall. "Do you have any idea how it felt to walk up to my home and see a For Sale sign in the yard?"

He furrowed his brow in obvious dismay and sat at the kitchen table, nodding to his wife that he wanted some coffee. They apparently had their own private language down, because she understood at once and poured him a cup.

"Where's this coming from? We've made no secret of the fact that we didn't plan to stay here."

"I didn't know it would be today. Nice welcome-home present, there."

"I apologize for not warning you, Katie. I planned to tell you last night, but you went over to Lindsey's so soon after you got back that I didn't have the chance."

She'd just gone over to her sister's to say hi, but then she'd gotten involved in a conversation with Lindsey and Zach about his grandma and the toll her Alzheimer's was taking. Not just on Grandma Rundle, but on the whole family. When Katie had finally looked at her watch, it was after ten and her dad and his wife had gone to bed.

She'd been relieved, actually. Not because she'd expected any kind of announcement about the house, but because she still wasn't used to her father being married to another woman. She would *never* be used to that.

"Katydid, Claudia and I are moving. We've found a much smaller house that we both like and we've put an offer on it. As soon as this one sells, the new one will be ours."

"I don't understand how you can sell this place." She sat down on the chair across from him, arms crossed, hating the emotion that made her voice crack. "We've lived here practically since I was born." She looked around at the walls, the floral wallpaper, thinking it was all so familiar that she'd never really noticed the details of it.

She didn't dare say this was her mom's house, because as uncomfortable as she was with her dad's marriage to Claudia, she wasn't out to hurt her. Until he'd gone and fallen in love with her a year ago, Katie had cared about Claudia just as much as everyone else did. It was harder to be welcoming now, but she made an effort not to be mean and not to let her know how much it upset her.

"This has been a good house for our family, but now our family has changed. And it's time for other things to change, as well. What could Claudia and I possibly need four bedrooms for?"

"It's nice to have my room back when I come home." Sometimes she felt as if her room here was more "home" than the bedroom in her apartment in St. Louis.

"We have a spare bedroom just for you at the new house. You can even help us decide how to decorate it."

She couldn't bear to think about being a third wheel in their new house. She couldn't care less what color they painted the walls. She'd be more comfortable staying in a hotel in Topeka.

"Why are you so against this, Katie?" her father asked. "You don't come home more than a handful of nights a year."

Katie leveled a look at Claudia, hesitating to get into this with her present. "Can we talk alone, Dad?"

"Honey, Claudia's my wife now. She's part of the family."

"It's okay," Claudia said. "I need to finish tidying up the bedrooms, anyway. Just in case we get a call to show the house." She glanced at the sign by the back door, as if to say that wouldn't happen without the sign being returned to the yard. Which, of course, was Katie's hope, regardless of whether it was rational or not.

Claudia left the room and went upstairs.

"This is Mom's house, Dad. How can you just sell it off?"

"It's been fourteen years since she died. How can you ask me not to? Do you really think that's fair to Claudia?"

Katie shrugged, knowing full well she

was acting like a sullen child but unable to stop herself. There was too much at stake here to just walk away without making her feelings known.

"Do you really think selling it's fair to the rest of us?"

Her dad leaned an elbow on the table, pinching the bridge of his nose with his fingers. "I'm afraid I still don't understand, Katie. Why are you so upset about this?"

She jumped up and began to pace. Part of her knew what she was asking for was unreasonable, but there was the other part, screaming out for her to do something about it. Begging her to do everything in her power to keep the house in the family. If she had the extra money, she'd buy the thing herself, just to have it whenever she came back to Lone Oak.

"I'm just…attached to it. Okay?"

"I can see that. I never realized you felt this way. You trucked on outta town the day after you graduated high school and barely stayed at home *before* that. I never would've guessed you had any affection for anything here."

It was clear in that instant that he included himself in the list of things she apparently hadn't cared about. She was sorry for that. That hadn't ever been the message she'd intended to send. In fact, she hadn't been trying to send any message at all. She'd just been coping, as best she could, with an event that had rocked their family in so many ways that they were still uncovering the effects.

Her mother had been the heart of the family, and when she'd been killed by a drunk driver each of them had flailed in his own private way. Katie's method of dealing with her pain had been to get out and live her life. It was still her method today. Whenever she caught herself feeling down about her mom—or anything else, for that matter—she sought out an adventure to prove just how much she was *living*.

"Talk to me, Katydid. Make me understand."

Talking about it made her squirm, but

so far *not* talking about it had gotten her nowhere. She was going to have to try to explain something she didn't fully understand herself.

She turned around, using the counter for support, unsure of what to say. "This house is where all my happiest memories are," she said at last. "Growing up with a mom and a dad and Lindsey and Savannah. We were a normal family that did normal things, happy things. Not the poor Salinger family who'd suffered an awful tragedy. Life was so good back then."

"It was." His smile was bittersweet.

"No matter how crazy my life gets now, no matter where I fly off to, I know I can always come back here to get that feeling of...*home*. Contentment. Happy family. Good memories. This is the only place in the world where I feel that way, Dad." She hugged herself. "And now you're going to sell it to the highest bidder."

He didn't say anything.

"I can still remember Mom here in the kitchen, rolling out cookie dough for us girls after school. She wore that awful apron."

Her dad chuckled softly. "The one with the rubber chickens all over it. Savannah gave that to her for her birthday one year."

"Savannah always did have horrible taste." Katie looked up, meeting his gaze across the room. "I'm afraid we'll lose all of that if you sell this place."

He stood and came over to her. Nudged her chin up with his knuckle, forcing her to make eye contact. "We won't lose any of that, Katie. We all have it inside."

She shook her head, tears filling her eyes. "It won't be the same." She took several steps away from him. "Look at the wallpaper. Mom spent hours hanging it. Lindsey and Savannah helped her and I had to sit at the table in the middle of the room, coloring pictures so that I wouldn't make a mess of the glue." She sniffled sadly. "Someone else will come in here and just tear the paper off without a thought."

"With good reason," he said, amused.

"I'm betting it's been out of style for ten years, at least."

Katie glared at his attempted levity. How could he be lighthearted when she was so upset?

He turned serious. "I have to do this. That part of my life is over, and my new wife shouldn't have to live surrounded by the memories of my first wife." He reached out and took her shoulders firmly in his hands, forcing her to look at him again. "I'm sorry, Katie, but I'm selling the house. The sign's going back in the front yard. If you don't put it out there again, I will."

He waited, eyeing her resolutely. Feeling defeated and knowing she couldn't win this battle, Katie went over to the sign and picked it up. As she focused on the handwritten phone number that had signified "home" for so long, her throat nearly closed on her. She hurried outside as the tears spilled down her cheeks.

CHAPTER TWO

NOAH PAUSED WITH the lawn mower running and pulled off his T-shirt to wipe the sweat from his face. Humidity was for the birds. He'd spent months without modern conveniences in the blistering heat of Africa, and he'd been fine. Three weeks back in the Midwest and he found that he wanted to weep like a baby any time he was out in the sun too long. What was wrong with him? He'd grown up mowing this gargantuan piece of land. He knew, though, that he wasn't the same as he used to be. Never would be again. While the damage from his time abroad was supposedly all psychological, he recognized a physical difference, as well. Or maybe he was just getting old. He *felt* old. Exhausted. Even though he was only thirty-six.

No matter how wimpy he'd become, though, he'd much prefer taking care of this task to letting his dad do it. Apparently, his old man had been handling all the lawn care by himself. Noah couldn't figure out what was going through the older man's head to make him think that was okay. He was almost retirement age and he had enough money to hire a full-time gardener if he wanted to. All Noah wanted was for him to stop the hardcore stuff, like lawn mowing. He could dig in the dirt to his heart's content. Even buying a riding mower would make more sense than pushing one over this huge lawn.

Noah winged his wet shirt onto the grass he'd already mowed and started down a new row when his mom caught his eye, waving like a possessed woman from the back door.

Not entirely upset at having to stop and take a break, he turned off the mower and strode toward the house.

"Miss me already?"

"Noah, the heat index is one hundred and four degrees. You're a doctor, for goodness' sake. You know it's not good to be out working in this weather."

"Want a hug?" He went toward her with his arms outspread, threatening to soak her in sweat.

She glared at him over the rims of her glasses as they walked inside.

"Speaking of working in the heat, once I move out we need to hire a lawn-care service for you and Dad."

"Have fun telling him that," she said. "He's the original lawn warrior. And if you even hint that he can't handle it anymore…" She shook her head sympathetically, as if he'd be a goner. "Lemonade's on the table. Sit down and have a drink."

"Dad's getting too old to mow." He looked for the pitcher. "Is it fresh squeezed?"

"Have you ever known me to buy that frozen garbage in a can?"

"No, ma'am," he said with the most sober face he could muster. To his mom, lemonade was serious business. It always had been.

"Well, then."

Noah washed his hands at the sink and bent over to splash cold water on his face.

"You should mow first thing in the morning, before it gets so hot. Not in the heat of the day after a full eight hours at work."

"I have a job first thing in the morning."

"The grass will wait till the weekend."

"It'll be a foot tall by the weekend. Mom, I'm young. Doing fine. I need the exercise." He sat at the kitchen table and poured lemonade from the old-fashioned pitcher into a tall glass. The familiarity of all this made him think, once again, how good it was to be back home.

"You need to relax. Take some time off. Stop working so hard, Noah."

"Work is good for the soul."

Martha Fletcher lowered herself to the simple oak chair next to him, the one she'd been sitting in for meals for as long as Noah could remember.

He couldn't keep himself from noticing yet again how much his parents had aged during the time he'd been away. Their wrinkles were deeper, their movements were slower, even if they didn't acknowledge it themselves. Noah shuddered at the thought of losing either one of them and hated the idea of them being old, even if he and his father had banged heads repeatedly as they tried to work together for the first time. He was still suffering from the loss that had crushed him less than a year before and he couldn't weather another one.

Unfortunately, his concern was mirrored in his mother's face. She gazed at him with worried hazel eyes. She hadn't changed the style of her straight bobbed hair for probably twenty years, but the color now was closer to white than gray. Her cheekbones were more pronounced, too. And she became bonier rather than rounder as the years passed.

Noah should be used to the look she gave him. She'd acted overly worried ever since he'd returned three weeks before. He'd tried to ignore it, hoping she would see that he was fine.

"Work might be good for the soul, but I'm wondering just where your soul is," she said after a thoughtful pause. "Where your heart is. It doesn't seem to be in *anything*, and that concerns me."

"Mom, please don't. You have to stop worrying about me." The irony of his own distress for her and his dad didn't escape him. But he supposed he was just at that stage in his life. What did they call it? The sandwich generation. Except he didn't have a wife and kids.

"You've always been the most passionate, involved person I know," she continued. "I love that about you, even though I used to be scared to death you'd get yourself in trouble caring so much."

"I'm fine. Tired and hot, but fine."

"If you're fine, then I'm a Hollywood actress."

Noah couldn't help it. He chuckled.

"Exactly." His mom remained unsmiling. "I wish you'd talk about what happened when you were away."

He pushed back his chair and stood,

wiping all signs of amusement from his face. "I need to get back to work."

She rose, as well. "Come on, Noah. I'm your mother, not the bad guy. Not some psychiatrist who wants to analyze you. Did it ever occur to you that talking about it might help?"

He looked at her for several seconds without really seeing her, terrible memories hammering at him, images of a dying woman etched into his mind. His throat seemed to swell shut and the familiar pain at the base of his neck edged into his consciousness. "No. It didn't. And no, it wouldn't."

It would only make her worry more, and what Noah wanted to do was ease his mother's mind, not fill it with horror.

Her shoulders sank and she stepped out of his path, looking defeated. He really hated making her feel that way.

He paused next to her and leaned down to meet her gaze. "You're prettier than any of the Hollywood actresses I've seen."

"You're full of it, Noah. Go mow the lawn. Dinner will be ready in an hour."

He frowned as he headed back out into the relief of the choking heat. At least the humidity didn't induce guilt or the paralyzing fear of losing someone he loved. Again.

IT WAS AFTER ELEVEN when Katie woke up. That was late enough to embarrass even her, but she'd crashed hard the night before and hadn't set an alarm. She changed into shorts and a T-shirt and pulled her hair back, promising herself a shower just as soon as she'd made an appearance and gotten some breakfast.

The main floor was deserted, but she heard voices coming from the basement. After filling a bowl with Rice Chex—she really needed to hit the grocery store for some decent sugar-filled breakfast alternatives—she decided to see what kind of party was going on down there.

She clomped down the wooden plank stairs all the way to the unfinished basement. The familiar smell of dust and mustiness took Katie back more than a decade to when she and her sisters had played down here. The closet under the stairs had been the headquarters for their members-only club and Savannah and Lindsey had been typical tyrannical co-presidents. When Katie had finally gotten tired of being the club gofer, she'd formed her own club and had convinced her mom to become the only other member.

Katie smiled at the memory, then it struck her again that moments like this were on their way out of her life. Sure, she would still have those memories, if she strained her brain. But just walking around this house brought back so many good times that she knew she'd never think of otherwise.

"Good morning," Mrs. Hale—*Claudia*—said from behind a pile of boxes. "I hope you slept well. Your dad was going to wake you before he went to work, but I figured you needed the rest if you were still asleep."

"Morning," Katie said, straining to be

friendly. "Thanks. I guess I was tired. I always sleep extra well here."

"About time Sleeping Beauty showed up to help." Savannah emerged from behind another tower of boxes and headed toward Katie, arms outstretched.

"About time you came by to say hello." Katie smiled and wrinkled her nose as they hugged. "Thanks for the dust bath."

The middle Salinger sister hadn't changed much in the months since Katie had last been home for a visit. Her auburn hair was pulled up sloppily and her eyes showed fatigue. Part of being a mother to two kids, Katie guessed. The amount of dust on Savannah's black yoga pants and old Hard Rock Cafe T-shirt made Katie's nose itch.

"The kids have been dying to see you, but we spent a good chunk of the day yesterday at a museum in Topeka with some of Logan's friends."

"Where are the kids?" Katie asked, looking around. She could hear their voices, but there were so many places to hide in the basement that she couldn't even tell which direction the noise was coming from.

"They're in the other room, looking for the boxes of toys that Mom packed away."

"Oh, I have dibs on my G.I. Joe stuff!" Katie headed into the back room of the basement, groaning as she imagined going through all the boxes in order to prepare for the move.

"Hey, guys," she called out to the kids, who were engrossed in the contents of a plastic storage bin.

Her niece and nephew ran to her and attacked her with fierce hugs, making her laugh.

"I heard you're searching for toys," Katie said.

"Grandma said there might be LEGOs!" Logan hopped back to where they'd been rummaging through a large box. The adorable round-cheeked boy rarely just walked anywhere.

Katie paused momentarily at Logan's use of *Grandma,* referring to Claudia. Yet another thing she needed to get used to if she was going to hang around here for a while. Up till now, she'd mostly been able to avoid the impact of her dad's marriage. She shook her head to bury her thoughts.

"From what I remember, you already have enough LEGOs to build a small house," she teased.

"I want to build a big house!"

Katie laughed and went over to hug him again. "How's it going, Allie Cat?"

"Okay." Her lanky niece smiled, her brown eyes twinkling.

"You looking for LEGOs, too?" Katie asked, motioning her closer with her good arm. Allie was on the shy side, but irresistible with her curly brown hair pulled into a ponytail and a smattering of freckles across her cheeks.

"No. Just looking for anything that's neat."

"It's like a treasure hunt, isn't it?"

Katie turned around and began scavenging, one-armed, through the boxes behind Logan, not sure what to expect. Her mom had had a reputation for saving *everything*. Judging by the number of boxes, bins and bags filling most of the basement, Katie doubted anything had been touched since long before her mother's death.

She pried open the cardboard flaps on the top box, stood on her toes and looked in. The first thing she saw brought a nostalgic smile to her face and she pulled it out. She removed a clear plastic bag, inside which she could see her beloved stuffed polar bear, clean and safe from harm. She opened the bag and took him out.

"Aww," Allie said. "Can I see him?"

Katie hugged the bear briefly and then handed him to Allie, who'd sidled up next to her. "His name is Ozzie. He's a very important bear."

Allie cuddled him in her arms.

"He'd be happy to have someone love him again. Think you're up for the job?"

"Yes!"

Katie wasn't sure she'd ever seen such a big smile on her niece's face. "Keep him safe for me, will you?"

"I'm gonna show my mom." Allie walked off, cooing to the bear and explaining in a soft voice that he was going to a new home.

"I want something, too," Logan said.

"Logan, my friend, judging by the number of boxes down here, I have a feeling we could fill your entire bedroom with somethings."

Katie rose onto her toes again, to see what else was in the carton she'd opened. A couple of other less-cherished stuffed animals were on top, similarly packaged. She took out a black Lab puppy and showed it to Logan. "Want to adopt a dog?"

"Sure! Does he have a name?"

Katie thought for a minute, trying to recall. "Willowby."

Logan studied the dog. "Can I give it a new name?"

"Yep. But it might take him a while to learn to answer."

He glanced up at her, confused. Finally,

he seemed to grasp that she was kidding and giggled.

Katie returned her attention to the box. Removing a tattered stuffed rabbit, she could better see the remaining contents: a collection of colored headbands, a photo album, a ballerina music box, an oversize accordion file full of schoolwork, a small jeweler's box.

She pulled out the box, vague memories flickering at the edges of her awareness. She opened it and gasped, then rubbed her loosely fisted hand along her bottom lip, back and forth.

"What's that?" Logan asked, peeking around from behind.

"A necklace. My mom gave it to me."

When had it been? Her tenth birthday, she thought. The silver heart had a deep purple amethyst set into its right side, and it dropped from a delicate chain. Katie hadn't worn it more than two or three times, she recalled, declaring it too girlie.

"It's pretty," Logan said, his voice full of innocent reverence. Then he skipped away. "Gonna show my mom my new dog."

Katie hardly heard him, deeply engrossed in memories as she was. Had she hurt her mother's feelings by refusing to wear the necklace? Pain constricted Katie's chest and moisture filled her eyes, the guilt she'd been exempt from years ago hitting her now. Taking out the necklace and tossing the tiny box back inside the carton, she unclasped the chain and pushed her hair to one side so she could put it on. She struggled, but finally felt the slight weight of the charm settle on her breast bone.

"I'm sorry, Mom," she whispered, running her fingers over the heart. She made the decision, at that moment, to wear the necklace as much as she could. She actually liked it now. In fact, it was almost a match to her belly ring. She wondered if that had been some kind of subconscious thing on her part.

As Katie dug into the box again, to see

if there was anything else of interest, she heard loud footsteps in the kitchen above from near the back door. Men's footsteps, which told her her dad had come home for lunch.

But he wasn't alone. If she wasn't mistaken, there were two men up there. She wandered back out to the other room.

"Are you expecting someone?" she asked Claudia, who was hunched next to Savannah and Allie as they flipped the pages of an old photo album.

Claudia looked up, belatedly noticed the noise upstairs and stood. "Oh, my goodness. Yes. Your dad was bringing someone by to look at the house."

Already? "That was fast. How did anyone even find out about it so quickly?"

"It's Wednesday in Lone Oak, Katie dearest," Savannah said. "Newspaper day. If you'd been up in time to look through it, you'd know there's an ad in there for the house."

Katie stuck out her tongue at her sister.

Claudia was making her way to the

kitchen. "Allie, Logan. Why don't you kids come up and play outside while we have guests."

Logan ran up the stairs noisily. Allie looked at Savannah. "I'd rather stay down here with you."

"That's fine, sweetie."

"Wonder who the circling shark is," Katie said, touching the locket around her neck.

"No idea. Why don't you go check it out?"

"Aren't we supposed to be gone when people go through the house?"

Savannah shrugged, still going through the pages of an old picture album. "Look how cute you were. What happened?"

"Aww," Allie said. "That's Aunt Katie?"

"When she was brand, spanking new. Look at that red face."

Katie walked a few steps closer to see the photograph. Her mom lay in the delivery-room bed, holding a tiny baby bundled in a pink and yellow blanket. "I was cute. Still am, much to your mother's dismay," she said to Allie. "I'm going to investigate. Maybe I can scare away the potential buyer."

"I have no doubt you probably can," Savannah said with a grin. "I'll just be down here slaving away."

Katie rushed up the stairs. She could hear her dad's voice, along with another one, in the living room. A vaguely familiar voice that she couldn't quite place.

When she poked her head around the doorway between the kitchen and the living room, the mystery was solved. The shark was none other than Dr. Fletcher, of the grumpy younger variety.

"Hello, Katie," he said. "I wondered if you two were related."

"Katie's my youngest daughter," her dad explained. "You two know each other?"

"Dr. Fletcher had to resew my stitches yesterday."

"Resew them?" her dad asked. "What happened?"

"Nothing much," Katie said. "I fell while I was skating. Popped the old ones."

"And you didn't tell me?"

"I'm on my own health-care plan. What did it matter?"

Her dad stared at her, speechless. "I just would've thought getting stitches warranted a small mention."

"I wasn't in a talkative mood last night. Be sure he tells you all about the leak in the ceiling of my sister's room," she said to Dr. Fletcher before heading outside to see what her nephew was up to.

"It's all in the disclosures, dear daughter of mine."

"Perfect. Then there won't be any problems." Katie walked out without saying goodbye.

Too bad she didn't really believe that. She was having a serious problem with the idea of Dr. Fletcher—or anyone else—living in *her* space. She'd known last night there was nothing else she could do. She even understood her dad's reasoning and could admit it made sense.

But for all the telling herself everything would work out fine, she was sure having a big problem believing it.

CHAPTER THREE

JOGGING WAS A SORRY substitute for the rock climbing Katie normally indulged in when something was bothering her or when she simply wanted some exercise. The thing about rock climbing was that not only did it give her a great workout, but she had to concentrate fully on what she was doing the whole time. Jogging, not so much.

Running didn't occupy her mind and it didn't allow her to forget her problems. But something about the pounding of her feet on the paved trail at least gave her the illusion she was working off steam. The path wound along the riverbank, hugging its curves, and it was shaded by towering trees on both sides. But the beauty and serenity were lost on Katie at the moment.

Gritting her teeth, she pushed herself to speed up. She glanced at her sports watch as she spotted another mile marker and realized she was keeping better than an eight-minute-mile pace. She very rarely ran and she knew she'd pay for this tomorrow. No matter how in shape she was, jogging always made her hurt in places she'd forgotten she had muscles. She pressed on anyway.

After she'd gone three miles, she dropped to a walk while she caught her breath. The running wasn't making her feel much better at all.

A giant boulder jutting out over the riverbank tempted her. She couldn't resist climbing onto it to watch the lazy water. And breathe.

The trail was mostly deserted this evening, which was fine by her.

Katie fiddled with a pile of small stones that someone had left atop the boulder. She sat and watched as a pair of swallows swooped down to skim the water's placid surface.

Four miles and she still couldn't get the loss of her mother's home out of her mind.

Her chest tightened and a lump formed in her throat. She'd been teetering between burning anger and deep sadness for the past twenty-four hours and the swing of emotions was exhausting.

She reached for the pendant that hung against her collarbone, running her fingers over it lovingly.

The sound of another person coming down the trail drifted into her consciousness. She straightened a bit, picked up one of the stones and skimmed it out onto the water as the jogger neared her spot.

Something made her turn to look. Recognition reflected in his eyes at the same moment it hit her.

"Katie?" He came to a stop at her rock.

"Dr. Fletcher." The T-shirt he wore—white, with a red Medical Missions emblem on the chest—revealed a set of biceps and pecs that up until now had been unseen. She would've noticed *those,* she thought distractedly.

"Call me Noah," he said, propping one foot on the far edge of her rock. He wasn't even breathing hard. "You're a ways from home."

The mere mention of home was enough to make his muscles cease to matter. "Home seems to be a relative term these days." She couldn't help the unfriendliness in her voice. Didn't want to.

He glanced down the trail, then looked back at her as if he were making a decision. "Mind if I join you for a minute? I could use a rest."

She shrugged and moved over on the rock. "You're not even out of breath. I take it you run a lot," she said, looking out over the water.

"Every day. Sometimes twice."

That was fitting. "Weights?" She glanced at his arm muscles again, then dragged her gaze back to his face, noticing the angles of his jaw and his sandy five-o'clock shadow.

"Some. You?"

Katie shook her head.

"Weights aren't exciting enough?" There was a hint of disapproval in his voice.

"Got something against excitement?"

He looked directly into her eyes for the first time since he'd stopped. "It depends on the circumstances."

She skipped another stone before Noah helped himself to the pile between them and sent one of his own skimming—three jumps—after hers. She narrowed her eyes and concentrated, then skimmed another, frowning when it refused to go more than three skips.

"You run much?" he asked.

"Only when I can't do something better."

"What would you rather do?"

"Climb rocks."

"I can see why that wouldn't work right now." He glanced at her cast.

"You going to buy our house?"

"I'm thinking pretty hard about it. Is there any reason I shouldn't?"

"It's too big for you."

"How do you know I don't have a family?"

"You don't have that gets-along-well-with-others look about you. And also no ring."

Noah stared at her for several seconds, considering whether to argue, then deciding to ignore the insult. He couldn't help noticing her profile was well-proportioned—full lips, dainty nose, thick lashes. A small but deep scar marred the left side of her forehead, the only imperfection in her smooth-looking skin. He was afraid to guess what had caused it. She needed to take better care of herself.

"I want to see the house again."

She closed her eyes for a moment. Between that brief look just now and her comment about the leaky ceiling when he'd gone through the house, he was starting to suspect she didn't want him to buy her dad's home. He couldn't worry about that, though. Moving out of his parents' place was a priority; he had to do it while he still got along with them. If he decided the Salinger house was the best for him, Katie would just have to get used to the idea.

Noah climbed down onto the path and bent to tie a lace that was loose.

Katie sent another small smooth stone skipping over the water before jumping from the high end of the boulder down to the dirt—a good four-foot drop. He cringed, thinking about her numerous injuries.

"You heading back?" she asked, slapping the dust off her hands.

When he straightened, he took in her tight, flat stomach—revealed between spandex running shorts and a hot pink sports bra—and the piercing of her navel. He struggled to pry his eyes away from it, tried not to think about how that delicate piece of jewelry was capturing his attention as none had before.

"It's an amethyst and a heart," she said.

"What?"

"Aren't you staring at my belly ring?"

"No." Yes.

"So... Coming or not?"

He considered going another mile, which was what he normally did, but he'd lost momentum sitting here. It'd be dark soon.

"Why not." He gestured to the path toward the city park and Katie started running. In front of him. He tried to ignore the way she looked in running shorts that revealed long, muscular legs.

They jogged for a few minutes without speaking. The only sound was the pounding of their feet on the pavement.

"How can you stand to run so much? Twice a day?" Katie asked finally, breathing hard.

"Want to slow down?"

"No. That's not what I mean. Just… It's monotonous and painful and possibly the most boring exercise on the face of the earth."

"You adjust to the pain—and running can be meditative. It keeps me from thinking too much."

"Ah." She nodded, hesitated, and he thought she was trying to catch her breath. "Africa?"

He faltered, lost his footing, jarred by

the mere mention of it. Most people didn't have any notion of what he'd been through. The few who did didn't have the nerve to bring it up, and that was the way he preferred it. "What do you know about Africa?"

She'd slowed, too, and now she stared at him. "Not much. I've just heard stories floating around."

He wished he could tell the women at the clinic not to discuss his past or his personal life without coming off as a pompous jerk. "It's not much of a feel-good story."

"I heard you got shot."

His blood turned cold, but he forced himself to pick up his pace. "Yeah."

The seconds stretched out and Noah fought to keep his mind blank, using all his mental energy to push away those images before they took over.

"Just…yeah?" Katie asked.

He nodded.

"Is that an 'I don't want to talk about it'?"

"You catch on quickly." He wished he hadn't stopped when he'd seen her.

"I noticed the scar on your leg, when you were sitting next to me. It looks bullet-sized. Or what I would guess is bullet-sized, since I don't have a lot of experience with bullets making holes in legs. Am I right?"

"If I answer that question, will you let the whole thing drop?"

"For now."

Now was all that mattered to him, because he had no intention of spending more time with her. "Yes. I was shot in the back of the leg by a group of insurgents. What you saw was an exit wound."

"Wow. Did you…"

"You said you'd drop it."

"Sorry. It's not every day I meet someone who's been shot."

Even that brief exchange put his nerves on edge. The tension in his shoulders and neck increased at least another ten notches and his body moved stiffly.

A few minutes later, Noah had loosened

up somewhat. He'd gotten good at ignoring everything other than the simple act of running, at turning his thoughts off all the way.

As they approached the park, Katie let out a loud whoop, startling him out of his tentative calm. She bent forward dramatically, stretching and feigning exhaustion. Or possibly not feigning at all. Her face was pink and she gasped for breath.

Noah went through his usual cool-down routine, walking in circles, gradually slowing his pace, stretching his back. The sun had fallen below the horizon, but the sky still held the last bits of light, forming a dark silhouette along the tops of the trees. Crickets chirped their summer song, luring him further into calmness.

Noises over in the playground attracted his attention. Katie grabbed hold of the merry-go-round, pushing it in a circle as she ran around the outside. When she'd picked up speed, she hopped on then sprawled on her back, feet toward the center, head on the outside edge. Her hair blew over the side, flying behind her.

Noah stood there, staring. What he really wanted to do was walk directly to his Tahoe SUV and drive home. But there were no other vehicles in the parking lot, so it appeared Katie might need a ride. He hadn't been raised to leave a woman alone in a park at sundown.

He took his time reaching the playground area, watching her spin as if she didn't have a care in the world. He couldn't relate at all to the concept.

"You're slowing down," he said when he reached the moving merry-go-round.

She laughed as she whirled past, then pulled herself up with her good arm and stuck out a foot to stop. Standing, she eyed him, her smile fading. "I don't suppose you want to go for a ride?" She started running in a circle again, jumped on the same way she had before, and was lying down before Noah could blink.

He couldn't imagine himself running

wild like that. He took a step back, waiting for her to slow down.

"Actually, I came over here to ask if you want a ride home."

She didn't answer right away. When the thing had nearly stopped spinning and Noah's patience had just about run out, she sat up.

"No, thanks. I'm going to go for a few more spins and then I'll walk home."

"You were ready to collapse ten minutes ago. You've got a broken wrist. You shouldn't push yourself anymore."

"You sound like a doctor."

The way she said it made it obvious that it wasn't a compliment. Noah wondered why he was wasting his time.

"Have it your way. Good night." He headed to the parking lot, thankful, after all, that she'd turned him down and he could drive home alone.

LATER THAT NIGHT, the house was so quiet, Katie thought she might climb the walls. Her dad and stepmom had gone to bed a few hours earlier. She'd flipped through a couple hundred channels on satellite TV and had found nothing that held her interest for longer than a minute. Then she'd dropped by Lindsey and Zach's house, next door, but it was clear they wanted to go to bed, so she left.

She sat at the kitchen table tapping her fingers on the surface. Seconds later she jumped up and opened the refrigerator, but she didn't see anything appealing in there. Remembering she'd left her laptop in the living room earlier, she retrieved it and returned to the kitchen table, plugging it into the phone outlet.

When she had a connection, she opened her browser and checked all her usual sites—mostly bulletin boards for extreme sports enthusiasts—cursing the pokiness of dial-up internet. She wasn't tempted to participate in any online discussions, so she headed to her in-box and sifted through her emails, answering a couple of them. She'd never thought about how many of her emails were work-related before. Now that she was on leave, her traffic had slowed way down—just when she needed interaction and conversation the most.

Katie grabbed a box of fish-shaped crackers from the cupboard and then parked herself back at the table.

Without really thinking about what she was doing, she found herself entering "Dr. Noah Fletcher" in a search engine and waiting nervously to see what popped up. Even though she had no earthly reason to be nervous.

Several links appeared and Katie paused, asking herself what she was doing. Between having Noah threaten to buy the house and seeing the evidence of him having been shot, her curiosity was piqued and then some. Still…she debated closing the browser.

Nah. What fun would that be?

She clicked on the first entry and the website for Medical Missions loaded. An article detailing the organization's efforts in the Democratic Republic of the Congo appeared and Katie began to read it, shuddering at the description of the situation in central Africa. She skimmed the article, looking for a mention of Noah Fletcher, but didn't see one. Then she noticed the photo. Was that him? She clicked to enlarge it and read the caption.

"Dr. Noah Fletcher arrives at the Medical Missions camp carrying a malnourished ten-year-old girl who'd been severely beaten. Dr. Fletcher was shot in the leg during an altercation with rebel forces but still managed to carry the young girl to safety."

Now that Katie looked again, she could tell it was him, but he was in such bad shape. Dirty. Exhausted. Eyes glazed with terror. No wonder, though.

Katie sat and stared, feeling more than a little shell-shocked herself. Her mind spun with the possibilities of what might have happened to him. The journalist in her wanted to know more. Why had they shot him? How had he rescued the girl? Who would hurt such a young child?

Was this the reason for the bone-deep

weariness radiating from his eyes? An explanation for his inability to smile?

Katie looked for links for more information, but saw none. She did a search on the Medical Missions site itself, but only turned up his media profile. No details on his accomplishments or on anything else he'd done for the organization.

She went back to the search engine results and clicked on every link listed. He'd apparently spent some time on the East Coast and had been part of a family practice there before volunteering. But that's all she found. A few listings on other medical sites, but nothing that told her more about what she wanted to know. About what happened in Africa.

She shut her laptop in frustration. Based on that one photo, it appeared Noah Fletcher was a real hero.

She began to see him in a different light.

It didn't mean she liked him. His uptight, controlling ways were enough to make her eyes cross. But she could admit—however begrudgingly—that her respect for him had increased significantly.

CHAPTER FOUR

KATIE ROLLED OVER, instantly aware of two things. First, it was far too early to get out of bed. Second, if she didn't get out of bed now and do something about it, the wound on her chin just might explode.

The cut felt as if someone was taking a pin and pricking drops of acid into her skin. Her head throbbed, and she knew, without touching it, that her chin must be puffed up like a blowfish.

She flipped over and pulled a pillow over her head telling herself to go back to sleep, but that hurt, too. So she rolled to the edge of the bed and sat up, fairly unhappy with the world.

Still drowsy, Katie made her way downstairs to the kitchen to find some breakfast. When she saw that Claudia had picked up a family-sized box of Lucky Charms, she nearly wept with joy. Sometimes it was the small things that got you through.

She was bent over her bowl catching up on the contents of Lone Oak's weekly newspaper when Claudia came in.

"Morning, Katie." Then she did a double take. "My goodness, what's wrong with your chin?"

Katie shrugged. "Hurts."

"It looks like it does more than just hurt. We need to get you back to the doctor."

As Claudia spoke, Katie finally woke up enough to realize she was right. Still, she groaned. "No. No doctor."

"Honey, that's not something you can ignore. Why don't you get dressed and I'll take you in."

Katie finished chewing her cereal. "I'll drive myself."

Her tone was sharp, making confusion and hurt appear on Claudia's face, but Katie wasn't in the mood to back down.

"I can take care of myself. It's no big deal."

Claudia sat in the chair next to Katie.

"Katie." Tentatively, she touched Katie's forearm, and though Katie's instinct was to pull away, she didn't. "I know you're still struggling with the idea of your dad getting remarried."

Katie met her gaze but said nothing.

"I'm not trying to fill in for your mom, honey. We've always gotten along in the past and I know it's going to take you some time to adjust. I just hope we can get back to that comfort level we used to have."

Katie slumped in her chair, pulling her arm away at the same time. She was acting like a bratty twelve-year-old stepchild and she knew it. The thing was, she didn't dislike Claudia at all. She didn't blame her for marrying her dad and didn't even really blame him for marrying her. In her mind, she understood they were in love and were happy together, and theoretically she wanted that for her dad. It was just that her heart hadn't caught up with the logic. She couldn't force herself to swallow such a gargantuan change and go on as if nothing was wrong.

"Claudia, I'll get there… I hope. But I'm not there yet." She stood, shoveling one last bite of cereal onto her spoon. "I'll drive myself to the doctor and I'll be fine." She carried the empty bowl to the sink.

Claudia nodded, looking less than happy, but was wise enough not to push the issue.

Katie found the number for the clinic and dialed it on her cell phone as she made her way upstairs.

"Fletcher Family Practice." Eve's formal voice made her grin again.

"Hey, Eve. Katie Salinger."

"Hey, what's going on?"

"I need to get in to see a doctor this morning. My stitches are infected. Is there any way I could see Old Man Fletcher today?"

"What's that all about?" Eve asked nosily. "Seemed like you got along okay with Dr. Noah the other day."

"He doesn't like me. I'd rather see his dad."

"He doesn't like anyone. You're not special." Eve chuckled. "Seriously, though, I'm supposed to give all call-ins to Dr. Noah."

"Why? What if the patient requests his dad?"

"Well, I might be able to get away with it, but he'll find out. He checks a couple times a day. Doesn't trust me."

"So you'll get in trouble?"

"I wouldn't say that. If you request his dad, that's your prerogative, right?"

"That's my thinking. What's he trying to do? Take over the whole practice?"

"You noticed he likes control, did you? He claims it's because he doesn't want his dad working so hard. I promise you if Dr. Ivan Fletcher finds out, you'll hear the blowup from there."

"Wouldn't blame his dad a bit. I'd blow up, too."

"Okay. I'm writing you down for Dr. Fletcher, senior. But there's one condition. You've gotta fill me in on what's going on when you get here."

"There's nothing. Really. We just met up

on the jogging path last night and he disapproves of me and everything I do. I'm not in the mood for a lecture about how to live my life."

Eve chuckled again. "That's so not 'nothing.' Can you make it by nine?"

Katie glanced at the clock. Ten after eight. "Yeah, I'll be there. See you then."

She headed upstairs for a quick shower. If she had to go out looking like a swollen lobster, she was at least going to make sure she didn't smell.

KATIE SAT ALONE in a different examining room this time, feeling slightly sick to her stomach. It was all she could do to stay awake while she waited. When this was over, she planned on a very long date with her pillow. Her body ached, as if she hadn't slept at all the night before, when, in fact, she'd been asleep a bit after midnight. Early for her.

She reclined on the table, unable to resist any longer the temptation to lie down. Knowing Dr. Fletcher, senior, would be the one to walk through that door helped relax her enough to close her eyes and drift off.

When she opened them again, the first thing she saw was the back of a doctor washing his hands at the sink near her head. And if she wasn't mistaken, that was not the back of an older man. Katie raised herself up to a sitting position, rubbing her eyes and wanting nothing more than to go back to sleep.

Noah turned toward her, drying his hands on a paper towel.

"You're supposed to be your dad." She didn't look straight at him, keeping the puffy side of her face away from him.

"My dad is busy, and I didn't think it was right to make him busier just because you and I don't see eye-to-eye on a few things unrelated to your medical care."

She turned her head toward him with the idea of arguing more, but then his gaze slipped to her chin and she suddenly felt ugly and unsure of herself.

"Ouch," he said, moving closer to inspect it. "It looks like you didn't have such a good night."

She squeezed her eyes shut as he moved his hand toward her chin, anticipating jabbing pain from his touch. But his fingers rested beyond the wound, where her neck met her jaw. This was a gentle caress, somehow caring yet still professional. She was thrown by his apparent concern.

"I swear I've done everything you told me to."

He nodded, still inspecting the wound. "I did say you could jog, didn't I?"

"Go ahead. Get the lecture over with."

"It doesn't sound as if I need to. You know what I'm going to say."

"I'm bad. I ran too far, too hard. Of course, that was partly to keep up with you. I do too many wild things, don't take care of myself..."

"Nice start," Noah said, dryly. "You do need to take it easy so your wrist and chin can heal. However, I don't think your questionable tendency to chase after adrenaline rushes had anything to do with this wound becoming infected."

The admission pained him, she could just tell. But the reprieve was much appreciated.

He touched her forehead next, just for a second, then frowned. "You have a slight fever." Noah glanced at her chart. "One hundred point four, according to the nurse."

"Am I dying?" She was starting to feel like it.

Noah looked into her eyes, his own lacking the annoyance of the previous night. It almost seemed as if he really did care. If anything, it had to be in a professional capacity. "I think you'll live. We'll get some antibiotics started right away. That should clear it up, but you have to promise me you'll rest all day today."

"Would it surprise you if I said there's nothing I want to do right now more than sleep?"

"Probably not as much as it surprises

you." He actually looked a little smug at that. "I want you to go home and sleep."

"Not a problem."

"Here's the catch. When you wake up and think you feel a lot better, I still want you to keep resting."

She sighed.

"Katie, this isn't serious yet, but it could quickly escalate. The infection has gotten into your body and we need to get it out."

"Okay. I'll keep resting. Yay."

"I love an enthusiastic patient."

What he loved was issuing orders, obviously. He thrived on it, she could tell. Probably was still getting a kick out of taking over the appointment she'd made with his dad.

"I found a picture of you on the Medical Missions site," she said, perhaps in an attempt to get back at him, throw him off kilter.

He was writing a prescription, but the moment she said it his pen stopped. His jaw tensed, but he quickly resumed writing. "Why were you snooping around there?"

"Curiosity. Because you wouldn't tell me what happened. They don't provide a lot of information about what you did, but I get the impression it was pretty heroic."

His head tilted up to meet her gaze. "It wasn't heroic." His tone discouraged all argument—or at least it might have with anyone else.

"I saw the little girl you saved, Noah. You got shot and yet you carried her back to camp. I'd say that's the stuff of hero-ism."

He signed the prescription form, press-ing the pen against the pad so firmly that she thought it might snap. "You don't know any of what happened." He said it so surely that Katie wondered if anyone re-ally knew the story, if he'd ever told a soul. "Please don't say it was heroic."

"You're modest. That surprises me."

He stood abruptly, ripping off the pre-scription and holding it out. "It has noth-ing to do with modesty."

She studied him, wondering exactly what was going through his head. Clearly he felt strongly about the nonheroic bit, but why?

"Have you done any interviews?" she asked, already suspecting she knew the answer.

"No, and I don't intend to."

"You should think about it. It sounds as if it's quite a story. Everyone's looking for a hero—people love reading about them." She folded up her prescription and stuck it in the pocket of her sweatshirt.

Noah opened her file and jotted down a few final notes, ignoring her.

"I have connections at the newspaper," she continued.

That made him turn to look at her, his eyes hard.

"My dad? The editor? He can assign someone good to write it. Someone who won't screw up the story. I'd offer to do it myself, but I'm on vacation." She climbed down from the table, trying to act casual, even though Noah looked as if he might strangle her.

"Rest today. Call us if anything gets worse. Fever, pain, nausea… We'd need to see you right away."

"Probably would've been easier to let your dad handle this appointment, huh?" She grabbed her purse and walked out, feeling his eyes burning holes into her back.

"YOU'VE COME TO HAUNT ME." Katie opened her eyes wider, rubbing the sleep from them. She sat up on the deep-cushioned chaise lounge she'd been dozing on. She'd come out to the screened-in porch to read and *rest* and had apparently fallen asleep. Again. She'd crashed for practically the whole day.

"Actually, I came to look at the house again," Noah said, pulling up a lawn chair and sitting so that he faced her.

She stifled a groan, barely. "So go look. Buy it. Whatever." She adjusted the seat to a more upright position.

"I already looked, thanks. I've been here for almost an hour with your dad."

Wasn't that just fabulous. "Well, this is the back porch. See?" She waved an arm at the room. "Now you can go."

"Is that the magazine you work for?"

He motioned to the latest edition of *Rush* on the end table next to her chair. She'd finished reading it before drifting off.

"Yep. That's it. It's got my article on hang-gliding in it. Would you like it?"

"I don't want to take your copy. I'll pick it up somewhere."

"I have others. I always have others. Take it." She handed it to him.

"So. Did you want something?"

"I wanted to talk to you."

"I'm fine. I've rested all day. You can ask Claudia."

"Feeling any better?"

"I just woke up. Can't tell yet. Still hurts, though." She risked running her fingers over her chin.

Noah leaned forward and rested the side of his hand on her forehead. It took Katie by surprise, but her head was already against the chair back so she couldn't move. He was close enough that she could smell his scent, a combination of soap and man, and she was surprised to realize she liked it. Liked his touch, here, away from the sterile exam room.

"It feels like your fever is gone. That's good."

"You should start advertising house calls. Not many people do this anymore." She babbled to hide her physical reaction, which was growing stronger by the second.

"I'm afraid this visit is a little more self-serving."

He sat back in his chair and Katie lamented the loss of his closeness. This infection was really taking a toll on her body, making her loopy, she decided.

"Well?" she prompted when he didn't continue.

"I don't know how serious you were earlier about siccing a reporter on me."

"I was serious. I'm a writer. I know a good story when I see one."

"Please, don't pursue this."

The emotion in his normally controlled voice startled Katie, and she took a closer look at him. His eyes held their usual weariness, but she saw something else there, too. Lingering pain. Sorrow. She sensed he was fighting a battle by himself, in his mind, and she almost reached out to touch him. That reaction in her was so foreign that it frightened her. Getting personal wasn't something she'd ever been comfortable with. Normally, she'd crack a joke and increase her physical distance.

And yet here she was, restraining herself from the urge to touch him. Bizarre.

"I told you earlier, my actions in the Congo weren't heroic."

"Right." She leaned forward, hugging her legs and paying close attention.

"That wasn't just me being modest. My actions were *not* heroic." He swallowed hard, trying to keep talking calmly, without allowing the images to infiltrate his brain and shut him down.

"Can you tell me about it?" Katie asked gently.

Noah looked around nervously. "This isn't the time or the place. It's…not easy for me to talk about."

"Okay." Her curiosity was piqued, but something told her not to press too hard. "Will you tell me another time? I'd like to understand."

Just then her dad opened the back door. "Noah, my wife's got an oven full of brisket. Why don't you join us?"

"I was about to leave," he said, standing and walking toward the older man. "It's a kind offer, but I don't want to intrude on your family time."

"That's a bunch of baloney."

Noah smiled tiredly at her dad. "Okay, I'll get to the heart of the matter. My mom's not the most understanding sort when I don't show up for a meal at the last minute. I don't want to suffer her wrath, as good as the offerings here smell."

Her dad nodded. "Women. I understand. Gotta keep 'em happy or we'll pay. Let's do it some other time, when we can plan ahead."

"That sounds like a deal." Noah looked over at Katie. "You're going to rest, right?" Clearly, family-physician mode was more comfortable for him. *Much* more comfortable than discussing his mission work.

"Whatever you say, Dr. Fletcher."

"I'll just see myself out here," he told her father.

"Oh, come on in this way. I'll see you out properly. No need to steal off into the evening out the back door."

Noah shrugged and looked at Katie. "Good night. If you get worse, call the after-hours number."

"I'll be fine," she said, distracted. She was already trying to figure out a way to get him to talk to her later. Tonight, if possible.

CHAPTER FIVE

KATIE HAD A PLAN and it was time to act on it.

"I'm going for a drive," she told her dad and Claudia, who were finishing dinner. "I need to get out of the house."

"Are you sure that's a good idea?" Wendell asked her. "You need to rest. Get better."

"I've been resting all day, Dad. I'm going stir crazy. I won't be out for long."

She stood and took her empty plate to the sink.

"I've got homemade shortcake with fresh strawberries," Claudia said.

Sugar wasn't going to distract her tonight. Since Noah had left, she'd thought about nothing except him and his secret. She'd thought of so many possibilities that her head was spinning. She needed to get the real story, if for no other reason than her peace of mind. She'd never been good at blowing off curiosity. Maybe that was why she'd become a journalist.

"I might have some later—if there's any left." Katie headed upstairs to change clothes and freshen up a little. Lying around all day had made her feel sluggish.

She pulled on some denim shorts and an old tee that said Wild Child in faded letters. She brushed the bed-head tangles from her hair and pulled it up onto the back of her head, slipped on her favorite hot pink flip-flops and went out to her Jeep.

The park was mostly deserted, except for a mom and two little kids over on the swing set. And a rusting Tahoe in the parking lot. She vaguely remembered seeing it at the park the evening they'd jogged together.

The sun was low in the sky, so she shouldn't have to wait long. She sat on a bench at one of the picnic tables close to the entrance to the path, watching the mother with her children. Several minutes later, the threesome wandered off, no doubt making their way home.

Katie was glad to have the park to herself sensing that Noah wouldn't talk to her if anyone else was around. Even then, it likely wasn't going to be easy to get his story out of him.

She settled herself on the bench, stretching out and looking up at the pattern of leaves against the sky. She felt better than she had earlier in the day, but she was still wiped out, low on energy.

Several minutes later, as the sky was beginning to grow dark, she heard someone approaching from the running path. She sat up, trying not to crane her neck, not wanting to look too eager.

The second he spotted her, he moved from a hard run to a slow, stretching walk.

"Hey," he said as he exited the trail and came nearer to her table.

"You aren't actually out of breath, are you?" she teased.

"A bit. Pushed hard tonight." He stopped

in front of her bench, hands on his thighs, bending over slightly. Then he sat down on the bench next to her.

They remained silent for a couple of minutes while he recuperated.

"What are you doing here?" he asked. "You're supposed to be resting."

"I *am* resting. I was lying down until I heard you coming." She turned sideways, swinging one leg over the bench so that she straddled it.

"Feeling better?"

"Much. Just worn out. I think I could sleep for a week."

"Maybe you should." He leaned back against the picnic table, resting his elbows behind him. "You didn't answer. What are you doing here?"

"I wanted to talk to you some more."

He gave her a guarded look but didn't say anything.

"I'd like to know more about what happened. Not so I can call a reporter or anything like that. I'm just interested. I can tell it was traumatic."

"Traumatic. Yes, it was definitely that." He avoided looking at her, avoided talking, as he paid rapt attention to the world around them. He watched a robin hop along the grass, hunting for its dinner. When the bird flew away, he switched his attention to an ant crawling on the bench between them. He held his finger there and let the ant crawl onto his hand, turning it this way and that so the insect was always visible.

"Will you tell me about it?" she asked, her patience already challenged.

"Why do you care?"

"That's a good question. One I don't really have an answer to, other than to say that I can see it weighs on you. Every day. For some reason, you truly believe that saving a child's life wasn't heroic. And I'm skeptical that you can convince me of that."

"Why does it matter whether it was heroic or not? What's done is done. I'm not looking for praise or comfort or commiseration. I just want to forget about it all."

"Maybe telling me about it would be a step in that direction."

"Or maybe it would bring it all back, as if it just happened yesterday." He flicked the ant lightly off his hand and onto the ground. "It isn't easy for me to talk about. To anyone."

Katie remained quiet for a beat, restraining herself. She didn't understand why it seemed so important to know the story. She just knew it was important.

"I'd like to know," she said quietly, honestly. She didn't allow herself to think about whether this was wise or not.

Noah closed his eyes. He did want to convince her of a few things, mostly to protect himself. He wanted her to understand that his actions hadn't been heroic. Then maybe she would drop the whole thing.

"If I tell you, will you promise to give up the gung ho reporter thing?"

She studied him, her head tilted to the side, and slowly nodded. "I won't tip off a reporter, but I might still try to convince you to talk to one."

He could handle that. She'd never convince him to go public with his story, even if she tried until she turned blue in the face.

Noah sucked in air as if this were his last chance to breathe. Tension pulled at every muscle in his body. The positive effects of his run had long since disappeared. He leaned forward, resting his elbows on his knees.

"I was in a pretty dangerous area with the lead physician one day." He couldn't tell her why they'd been there or what their purpose had been without revealing more than he wanted to. "He and I ran into a group of rebels who didn't want us hanging around, so we split up, trying to get away without getting hurt. I came upon a young girl, lying by the side of the road, weak, not moving. What little clothing she had was tattered. She'd been beaten badly.

"At first I thought she was dead, but when I touched her to check for a pulse she stirred. I forgot everything else. I just had to get her back to the medical camp, where we could try to help her."

Noah covered his face with his hands. "The rebels had guns. Grenades. Knives."

"You were unarmed?" Katie asked.

He nodded. "Corps policy." He closed his eyes. "I couldn't see them, but I knew they were still watching me, daring me to help her. Using her as bait. I walked down the road away from her and waited, keeping an eye on her from behind a rock. When I thought I'd outwaited them, I snuck back. There was no cover where she lay, so I had to move quickly."

He stopped for a moment to compose himself. "I was afraid she'd die before I could do anything. Selfishly, I didn't want that on my conscience. Didn't want to have the memory of her, alone, dying slowly because I was incapable of helping her.

"So I picked her up, praying her spine was okay, since I couldn't check before moving her. She was semiconscious and her pulse was weak. She weighed almost nothing. I remember thinking that. *She's so light. I won't have any trouble getting her back to camp.*

"I was almost out of range when they opened fire."

"You were hit," Katie said in a quiet voice, barely keeping a lid on her own emotions.

"My right thigh. I didn't realize it right away. The pain was so bad it went numb. Then it burned. As if it was on fire."

"What did you do?" She moved closer on the bench.

"The only thing I could do. Kept going. I thought if I stopped, I'd be shot and killed. I was scared out of my mind." He sat up straighter, leaning back against the table again and clenching his jaw. "So you see, no bravery involved. No heroism. It was simply fear that motivated me. Fear for myself. Cowardice, really."

She shook her head. "Fear, yes. Cowardice? I don't think so."

"I've never been in so much pain in my life." And that didn't even begin to describe the emotional horror from earlier in the day.

"How far was it back to camp?"

"A mile, give or take. It could've been a lot worse."

He stared in front of him, remembering the day clearly, reliving it. "When I got back, when that photo was taken, I was so out of it that I barely knew my name. Two of my colleagues rushed to take care of the child. I remember that. Remember being thankful she was no longer my responsibility, because I couldn't do a thing for her."

"You'd already saved her life."

"They didn't realize I was injured at first. My mouth was so dry I couldn't speak. Then someone saw the blood. Things got blurry after that."

Katie moved closer still. She took one of his hands in hers, resting them on his leg. "If you're trying to prove to me you're not a hero, you've failed." She smiled sadly. "What you did… That was the best example of a hero I've ever heard."

He shook his head, ready to argue, but she held up her hand.

"Listen to me, Noah. You were scared out of your wits. You said it yourself. But what did you do? You risked your life to make sure that girl didn't lose hers. You did it because you felt you had to."

"I did have to."

"Not everyone would feel that way."

"Could you have left her lying there?"

"I don't know what I'd have done. I'm not so sure I wouldn't have just run for dear life."

"Don't look at me like that." He broke eye contact, focusing instead on their hands. He absently caressed hers with his thumb, thinking nothing of the intimate gesture.

"Like what?"

"Like you think you're right and I'm wrong. I'm not a hero, Katie. It doesn't matter what you say."

"Heroism isn't based on whether you're scared, Noah. You don't have to set out to be a hero. It's all about how you react in the heat of the moment. You do what comes instinctively, without ever thinking, 'Gotta do something heroic here.'" She paused. "You passed the test. A lot of people wouldn't have."

He stood, uncomfortable with her words. He realized now, the only way he could convince her how wrong she was would be to tell her the rest—what had happened to Leah just before he'd found the child. And he wasn't about to do that.

He'd set out to shut her down, but now she'd twisted things and was more certain than ever that he deserved some kind of award. The thought made him queasy, because it was so far from the truth. "I should go. It's getting late and you need to go home and go to bed."

"*Now* you're being a coward," Katie said with a half grin.

"Look, I haven't told many people that story at all." He straddled the bench, too, facing her. "It probably sounds strange, but I don't like people to know what happened. I don't like to talk about it. Other things occurred that day that I can't go into, but if you knew, you would change your mind about me."

Katie studied him closely wondering what else might have happened. Maybe he'd tell her that, too, later. For now, though, she'd have to be satisfied. It was obvious he wasn't in the habit of sharing anything about his African nightmare. "I'm not going to tell anyone any of what you said."

"You're not going to call the press, anyway? Or tip off your dad?"

"I said I wouldn't. For all the many faults you think I have, breaking my word isn't one of them."

"Thank you." He rose from the bench, clearly ill-at-ease. "I have to head out. Please go home and sleep some more."

"Right behind you," she said, not moving. Her mind was racing a hundred miles per hour, trying to process everything he'd said. "Noah…"

He stopped and turned toward her.

"Thank you for telling me."

He stared at her for several seconds, then nodded once and headed for the parking lot. Slowly, shoulders sagging.

Katie watched him unlock the Tahoe and climb inside. Heard the engine start, saw him back out and waste no time getting out of there.

She was reeling from his revelations. Her imagination was in overdrive as she replayed the story he'd shared. There was no doubt about it, he *was* a hero.

She didn't want to be impressed by anything he'd said, didn't want to gain respect for him. They weren't friends. They had nothing in common.

But she couldn't help herself. She saw him differently now. Understood a little better why he was uptight and serious. She felt empathy for him—how could she not?

Begging him to talk had been a mistake, she realized. Despite her curiosity, she didn't like knowing something that private about someone she didn't know well. It made her uncomfortable.

The only thing worse would be if she

let him in on something that was just as personal to her.

She rose, deciding to push Noah and his story from her mind and do her best to forget about all of it. It didn't concern her, and he didn't like her knowing, anyway.

They would both just pretend they'd never had this conversation.

CHAPTER SIX

"I AM GOING TO hang you by your ears, Noah David Fletcher." His mom called out to him the moment he shut the back door.

He really needed to move out of his parents' home, he thought for the hundredth time as he shuffled toward his bedroom. His run had worn him out on its own, then his conversation with Katie had drained him completely. His emotions had been thoroughly wrung out just by voicing one part of what he'd experienced in the Congo.

"What'd I do now, Mom?" he hollered. He wasn't even sure what part of the house she was in, but her threat had been loud enough he could've heard it from a boat on the river a hundred yards away.

She suddenly appeared in his doorway.

"Housekeeping services?" Her tone was that of a horrified, deeply insulted woman.

Noah cringed. He'd had every intention of mentioning that to her ahead of time, but apparently he'd gotten the days confused. "I thought they weren't supposed to be here until Friday."

"I don't care what day it is. *What* was that little stunt about, young man?"

He had to stifle a smile, hearing again the term she'd always used when he'd been in trouble. "Just trying to help, Mom. No one can keep this house like you do, but I just thought you could use your time on so many other things."

"That's one hundred percent hooey, Noah."

"Besides, while I'm living here, I should help with the chores. This was supposed to be my contribution, since I'm never home enough to do much." Not to mention, she was a little militant about keeping things clean. He never got the chance to help with anything because she'd already done it all.

Her mouth actually hung open, then she

shook her head. "Have you heard the term *overkill* before?"

"Would it be so bad for you to have a little help?"

"You think I'm some old lady who can't handle it anymore, don't you?"

He threw up his hands. "I think nothing of the sort." It wasn't entirely a lie. He *could* see a difference in how she handled things, how she'd begun to slow down. While he knew she was perfectly capable of running the house and taking care of it, he didn't want her to feel that she had to. Maybe it was irrational of him. But he didn't want her to work herself to death.

"You are to call the Helpful Housekeepers and tell them to keep their mops to themselves. I won't have anyone waltzing around my house cleaning up after my family."

"You can cancel it after I move out."

"And when will that be? I have half a mind to kick you out tonight."

That actually made Noah chuckle, which wasn't easy to do these days. His mom had to be the only person on the face of the earth to ever be ticked off about the offer of free maid service.

He slowly moved closer and then hugged her. "I love it when you try to act tough."

"Cancel them." Without returning the affection, she marched off to the kitchen to cook dinner. Noah considered hiring a cook, just for the fun of watching her get bent out of shape again.

He shut his door. Grabbing the magazine Katie had given him earlier that day, he headed for the bathroom and turned the water on for a shower. As he waited for the water to warm up, he flipped the pages until he found the article she'd mentioned. She was the author and also the subject of most of the pictures.

His eyes were drawn to the photos. Her hair was pulled back on her head with loose strands falling into her face. The later in the ride or jump or…whatever one called a hang-gliding session, the more random wisps of hair there were. Her face was free of makeup, her complexion smooth, soft-looking. She smiled and her eyes sparkled with excitement in just about every picture, even when she was floating above the earth with what looked like minimal control over her situation.

He began reading the article and was soon engaged by her writing, in spite of his distaste for the subject. After a few minutes, he turned off the shower and wandered back to his room, flopping onto the bed to keep reading.

When he finished the story, he paged through the rest of the issue, looking for other writing by or about Katie, but found nothing. So he turned back to the beginning of her article again. He skimmed through it a second time and had no trouble acknowledging the fact that she was a talented writer.

The truth of the matter was she scared him. Zest for life was one thing, but the activities she pursued in the course of her job were senseless and dangerous. He didn't understand for a minute why someone would actually seek out ways to flirt with injury or death. Wasn't there enough chance of that without trying to fly?

She was a contradiction. Intelligent, a gifted writer who had the knack of making you feel as if you were right there next to her, experiencing the daredevil stunt of the day along with her, and yet she didn't value her life enough to take care of herself and try to stay safe. She thought nothing of stepping off a cliff with some sort of winged contraption strapped onto her.

He didn't understand it. Didn't understand her.

And he'd unwisely confided in her a part of the worst day of his life. He regretted opening up at all. It hadn't convinced her that he was not a hero. Now she would act differently toward him—as if they shared a secret.

It was a puzzling situation. Obviously something had moved him to confide in her, despite the fact that he'd had no intention of doing so. He'd have to raise his guard if he ran into her again. He had no business getting any closer to this attractive woman who clearly lacked sanity and sense.

"WHAT IF YOU AND MICHAEL bought Dad's house?" Katie asked Savannah, trying to sound nonchalant. She sat cross-legged on the bed as Savannah rushed around her bedroom getting ready to go out. Savannah had always been contrary, and if she thought Katie really cared about something, she was generally inclined to do the exact opposite. Savannah dropped the silver hoop earring she'd been trying to put on and bent down to retrieve it. "Why would we do that?"

"Because it's the family house. Because Dad wants to move out."

"Noah Fletcher's already interested in it."

"Exactly." It made Katie's stomach hurt. It didn't matter how she felt about what he'd revealed to her. She still didn't want to see him move into *their* house.

"So…I don't understand the problem. Dad wants to sell. Dr. Fletcher may want to buy. How and why would that concern me?"

"You're jumping to conclusions that he'll buy it."

"There are exactly three houses for sale in Lone Oak—I checked. The other two are a tiny broken-down dump and an isolated farmhouse. If he wants to buy something normal, he'll grab ours."

Katie tried to keep the panic from showing on her face. "That's why you should move fast."

"I think I'm missing something here. Why would we want to *compete* with someone who wants to buy the house?"

"It's the Salinger home, Savannah. It's been ours for more than twenty years. Don't you think it should stay in the family?"

"If you're so in love with the Salinger homestead, why don't you shell out the bucks for it?" Savannah hurried off to the kitchen, apparently not taking Katie's suggestion seriously. Katie followed her.

She had given thought to buying it herself. Maybe even seeing if her dad would work out a rent-to-own deal, since she was in no position to plunk down a couple hundred big ones or even come up with a down payment. Mostly, though, it came down to the fact that her job, her dream job, was in St. Louis. Not Lone Oak. She didn't want to live here. There was nothing here for her *except* the house.

But she wanted to be able to come back when she needed to, wanted to have a home. A place where everything was so familiar that she could see it in her sleep.

"I live in St. Louis. You already live here. Already own a house. All it would mean for you is moving about three blocks away to a place with a lot more room. Not exactly a hardship." She hopped up on the kitchen counter. "Would you guys at least consider it?"

Savannah shot her an annoyed look. "No."

"Just like that? You won't even talk to Michael about it?"

"Katie, what is up with you? Why are you being so weird about the house?"

"I'm just trying to keep it in the family. Why is that weird?"

Spilling to her dad about her feelings had been bad enough. She wasn't about to share her anxieties with Savannah and endure the inevitable ridicule. Savannah had never needed any special bait to tell her how odd or emotional she was.

"It's a pile of wood and brick. Just a building, Katie."

Katie leaned her head against the upper cabinets. "I know you don't get it," she said quietly to Savannah. "I don't like seeing it go to strangers. It's our house. You won't even ask Michael?"

Savannah reached into the kitchen junk drawer and pulled out a babysitter information sheet that Katie already knew by heart. Then she turned around and leaned against the countertop, avoiding Katie's eyes, suddenly seeming unsure of herself. For Savannah, that was significant.

"It's not a good time for the two of us to make any major decisions."

Katie opened her eyes wider. "Are you two having problems?"

"Michael's got so much extra work right now, and the kids are keeping me busy with their activities…"

"Savannah. You didn't answer my question."

Savannah cracked a single knuckle. A sure sign she was upset. Between the knuckle and the avoidance, Katie wondered exactly what was up.

"Katie, I said it's not a good time. Don't go making it into a federal case."

Katie studied Savannah, noticed, again, the rings under her eyes, the look of fatigue that might be more than the usual mom-of-two-kids kind. Savannah saw her paying such close attention and turned away abruptly.

"The kids haven't had a snack yet, so be sure to give them one in a little while. Logan can't have—"

"Anything with dairy. I know, Savannah."

"Sorry. Habit."

"You going to tell me where you're going yet?"

"I have an appointment in Topeka. Two-thirty." Savannah took out a bag of trail mix, set it on the counter and slammed the cabinet door.

"Ah, yes. So if I need something, I'll just call the appointment place in Topeka."

"I have my cell phone, Katie." She pointed to the info sheet. "Doctor's office, poison control center, Dad and Claudia, my cell."

"Got it, Van. Everything but where you're going."

"Good." Savannah opened the back door. "Kids, I'm getting ready to leave. Aunt Katie's here."

Katie heard Logan heading to give Savannah a hug and a shouted "Bye, Mom!" from Allie.

When her exasperatingly secretive sister was gone, Katie went outside. Savannah had been her final hope for keeping the house in the family. She hadn't been optimistic, exactly, but she'd thought Savannah and her husband might at least consider it. Of course that had been before she had any inkling they might be having problems.

KATIE STOOD, hands on her hips to help her balance, surveying the street below her. It'd been years since she'd climbed up here on the roof of the house and she tried to remember why it had been so long. Most likely because she never spent that much time in one place.

She was well aware that her father hadn't meant for her to come up *here* when he'd asked her—emphatically—to leave the house during his conversation with Noah. But she was out of the way and she had no plans to sabotage the offer her dad expected Noah to make on the house. Nothing would stop it.

She'd tried to resign herself to it, but she couldn't help the flood of emotions that rushed over her whenever she thought about losing her mother's home. Sadness, definitely. Anger—at her dad, at his new wife. At the person buying it. Aka Noah. Why he thought he needed a four-bedroom house was beyond her, anyway. He was a bachelor.

Speaking of Noah… Katie watched his battered Tahoe pull up at the curb and waited to see him emerge. She figured he wouldn't even notice her up here, so she made no effort to hunker down and hide.

On his way up the driveway, with a folder of papers in his hand, he glanced up and did a double take. "What are you doing up there?" he asked.

"Hi to you, too." Katie took two steps down the slope, closer to the edge.

"Don't move! I don't want you to fall."

"I won't fall. And if I do, yay, I have a doctor already on the scene."

The look he gave her told her several things. One, he thought she was a lunatic to be up there—especially with a cast and stitches, both of which he looked pointedly at. And two, she scared him. He couldn't handle her penchant for physical risk. He actually looked a little green.

That could be fun to exploit, she thought, allowing herself a wicked grin. A way to rattle the man-in-control.

She took another step forward, then sat down on the edge of the roof, dangling her feet over the gutter. "I hear you're putting an offer on the house."

"You heard correctly. Hopefully, I won't need to make an addendum about roof repairs."

She laughed. "That was a joke, wasn't it?"

He didn't show the slightest twitch of a smile. "You go out of your way to track down danger, don't you?"

"I like excitement," she said simply. "Better hurry inside. My dad can't stand tardiness."

He gave her one more assessing look, as if to calculate the likely damage when she landed on the pavement below.

"Don't worry," she told him, pulling

up her legs and crossing them. "I've been climbing on this roof since I was twelve."

He shook his head as if she were a significant menace to society and headed toward the front door.

"THANK YOU, MR. SALINGER," Noah said as they both rose from the dining room table half an hour later.

"Call me Wendell, son. Let's cut the formalities. We've got ourselves a deal and now we can be friendly."

"You've got it."

"We'll plan on being out of here in three weeks. The twentieth, then. Assuming we can arrange the closing that morning."

A clunk on the roof, above them, had them both looking upward.

"What on earth?" Wendell said.

"Your daughter, I believe. Katie? She was up there when I arrived."

"That girl." He closed his eyes as he spoke. When he opened them, Noah saw an eerily familiar look of complete fear. "She's my wild one. Always has been."

"I guessed as much when she showed up to have her stitches resewn."

"The more upset she is, the crazier the stunts she pulls. When she's not injured, that is."

"Is that why she's up there? She's upset?" Noah asked, surprised and a little intrigued.

Wendell sighed and nodded. "She doesn't want me to sell the house. If I thought my wife would allow it, I'd go up there right now and try to talk her down. I know she's hurting."

"How does she get up there?" Noah asked, not liking the idea that had just flitted into his mind.

"She climbs up the tree in the backyard, inches out on the big branch, then hops over to the back roof."

Noah cringed at the thought. "Here I figured it was something simple, like crawling out an upstairs window."

"Oh, you can go that way, too. But Katie prefers the other. I'm gonna see if she'll listen to me from down here."

"You could leave her there until she comes to her senses."

Wendell sized him up. "I like the way you think, son. But if I ignored her and something happened to her…" The look in his eyes troubled Noah.

"If you don't mind me asking, why is she upset you're selling? She doesn't actually live in Lone Oak, does she?"

Wendell shook his head. "She lives in St. Louis. Works for that extreme magazine. Wasn't exactly what I had in mind when she told me she was majoring in journalism. She's a real good writer, though." He looked back at Noah as if he'd finally remembered the original question. "She still thinks of this as her mom's house. Doesn't want to let it go."

Noah looked at him blankly.

"Her mom was killed in a drunk-driving accident fourteen years ago. Katie was thirteen. That was when she took the concept of daredevil to a new level, matter of fact."

Noah's head throbbed as he imagined

what a mother's death could do to a young girl. He knew too much about loss himself. Spent every day plotting how to avoid experiencing it again. He was a psychiatrist's dream because of it and he was thirty-six years old, not twelve.

"I'm sorry to hear about that," he said.

"We've adjusted by now. Mostly." His eyes rose toward the ceiling. "I worry about her, though. She'd have a fit if she knew how much."

"It seems like you worry with good reason." He started toward the front door, then paused. "Would it help if I went up to talk to her?"

Wendell crossed his arms and studied him again. "I'd be mighty grateful, Noah. Maybe you could infuse some sense into that brain of hers."

Not likely. Noah wasn't sure what he could do, or what he was going to say to her. All he knew was that if he could do anything at all to alleviate this man's concern right now, he would. Fear for those you loved was awful to live with.

"You'd prefer the window route?" Wendell asked.

"Please." Noah never had been a tree climber, never mind the thought of trusting one single branch and then jumping the rest of the way.

Wendell led him upstairs to one of the back bedrooms. He opened the door and Noah followed him in, stepping over pieces of clothing strewn across the floor.

"She obviously got the message we were done showing the place and no longer had to keep it neat," Wendell said.

"Katie?" Noah guessed.

Wendell nodded. "She really is a good girl. Just has a few bad habits."

"Don't we all?"

Wendell went to the window and hoisted it up. "Be careful. She makes it look easier than it is."

Noah sat on the windowsill and wondered what on earth he was doing. Then he took another look at Wendell and swung his legs outside.

"What I wouldn't give to see her face," the older man said.

Noah climbed out nervously, gripping the roof and staying low. He looked around, hoping Katie was close by and he wouldn't have to venture out too far.

No such luck.

She was apparently still up front. Noah would have to get himself to the peak of the roof in order to see her. Hopefully he could talk to her from there, because the thought of easing downward didn't sit all that well with him.

He took it slowly, testing each step before he put his weight down fully. By the time he reached the peak, sweat covered his forehead.

The look she gave him when he said her name, though, made it worth the climb. Surprise, confusion and shock played upon her features.

"What are you doing?" she asked, scrambling up the other side toward him, as if she'd seen a ghost.

"Your dad wants you to come down."

"Of course he does." An exaggerated wide-eyed crazy look came over her face. "He thinks I'm out of control."

"I'd have to agree."

"Why are you sweating? It's a gorgeous day out here, not even eighty degrees yet."

He avoided looking down. "Climbing up on roofs isn't something I normally do."

"I feel so...special." Then her expression changed. "Oh, wow. You're afraid of heights, aren't you?"

"I wouldn't call it afraid, really. I'm just not wild about being up this high with nothing to catch me if I slip."

She stared at him as if he were nuts and he was beginning to think she might be right about that.

"Forgive me for asking, but why in the world are you up here then?"

Noah lifted one leg over the top of the roof, so that he was straddling it. That felt a little more secure. Then he took a long breath to steady himself. "I told you, your dad wants you to come down. I didn't think it'd be good for him to climb up here.

Also—" he looked into her expectant eyes "—he said you come up here when you're upset about something."

"What would I have to be upset about?" she asked flippantly, and if Wendell hadn't already told Noah about Katie's problem, he might've believed she actually was carefree and just there for a better view of the neighbors.

Katie walked along the top of the roof, hands out, using it like a balance beam. Just as he was about to ask her—nicely but firmly—to stop, she climbed onto the chimney, which rose another three feet.

Noah closed his eyes in abject terror as she lifted herself to a full standing position. She was truly out of her mind.

"Making you nervous?" she asked from above.

"Are you insane? Get down from there before you wind up dead."

"Whoa!" she hollered, and he snapped his eyes open. "Gotcha." She stood perfectly still, nicely balanced, watching him.

"Katie…" He wouldn't be the least bit

surprised if someday he read a news article about someone wringing her neck.

"Okay, okay. I'll come down if it'll make you feel better."

He closed his eyes again, but listened to her as she got back to the main roof and made her way closer to him. His teeth were clenched so tightly he barely noticed the pounding in his head anymore.

She sat next to him and touched his hand. "You're really white-knuckling it," she said. "Are you sure you don't want to go back down?"

He'd come up here for a reason, or so he'd told himself. What was that reason? He tried to erase the fear she'd just put him through with her chimney stunt, in order to remember. Ah, yes. Her own feelings, which she seemed to be so willing to deny.

Noah told himself to relax his body a notch or two and then sat up straighter. "Your dad said you didn't want him to sell the house."

Her expression changed, the taunting twinkle that had been in her eyes disappearing and giving way to a look of such intense sadness that he almost felt bad for bringing it up. Almost, but not quite.

"Yeah. So?"

So she wasn't the type to pour out her heart and soul. He could relate well to that and he didn't necessarily consider it a bad trait. Just something to prolong his time forty feet above the ground. Come to think of it, maybe it *was* a bad trait.

"He mentioned something about this being your mom's house."

She locked her gaze with his. "Why does it matter if I'm upset? Who cares why I climb trees and roofs?"

"Your dad, apparently."

"He's used to it."

"Do you think anyone really ever gets used to someone they love taking insane risks?" His voice carried more anger than he intended.

She stared at him. "I'm still trying to figure out why you thought it would be okay to come up here and tell me everything that's wrong with my life."

He counted to ten, regretting his words. He'd meant what he said, but still… He barely knew her. "I'm sorry. I've messed this up."

"Messed what up?"

"I have no idea." He moved his left leg so he faced the backyard squarely now and, more importantly, the window that was his escape hatch. "I didn't come up here to antagonize you. Let's just pretend I shook your dad's hand and walked out the door, straight to my SUV."

Noah inched his way toward the dormer window below. When he was halfway down, Katie stood straight up and walked by, nearly making him lose his grip as she passed. When she got to the dormer, she turned toward him. She stood there watching his every slow move, unnerving him.

When he was a few feet from her, she stretched her good hand out to him. "Grab on."

"I'm fine," he said and tried to speed up his descent until he, too, could hold on to the dormer.

"Fine and stubborn," she said, then crawled in through the window.

Closing his eyes, he climbed in after her. Once both feet were on solid hardwood, he let out the breath he hadn't known he was holding. He glanced at Katie, who was staring at him, and then started toward the door.

"Noah," she said, taking a couple steps closer. "I'm sorry I was rude. I don't like to talk about my mom, or the house, or any of that. And yes, I'm angry he sold it."

"The rude, I can handle. It's the stunts that age me ten years."

"You really are uptight, aren't you?"

"I like to call it sane."

"It was kind of brave of you to chase after me on the roof. Especially being afraid of heights and all…"

He sighed, wishing he'd not followed whatever wild notion it was that had made him go on the roof in the first place. Who did he think he was? Some modern-day knight in shining armor? Even if he was, Katie did not need to be rescued. At least not from the roof. "I'll never hear the end of it, will I?"

"Not likely." She walked to the door of the bedroom and opened it for him. "Tell my dad I'm fine."

"I think he'll do better hearing it directly from you."

"Bossy," he heard her mutter as she turned and closed herself in her room.

CHAPTER SEVEN

NOAH PAUSED BEFORE opening the door to Katie's examining room, bracing himself.

He was supposed to see her as a woman with stitches that needed to come out and nothing more. But what he noticed first when he looked at her was the bright orange-flowered sundress that hugged her body just so, the way her hair looked silky as it cascaded over her shoulders and the gleam of mischief in her eyes as she smiled at him.

"Good morning. Ready to get those stitches out...again?"

"Like you wouldn't believe. You can have the cast back, too, as far as I'm concerned."

"You're out of luck there. Just a few more weeks though."

She looked at him as if to say, *Easy for you to say*.

He glanced over the instruments laid out, making sure his nurse had prepared the ones he needed, and scrubbed his hands.

Katie had been on his mind ever since he'd left her the day before, and that bothered him. He couldn't stop thinking about the way she was still struggling with her mother's death, so many years after it had happened. Would he still be battling Leah's ghost fourteen years from now? He'd really hoped it would get easier.

He had concluded she didn't need someone to rescue her from the roof, but he sensed she needed something. Her daredevil acts seemed to him to be a call for help, however subtle, possibly even subconscious. Her dad had said she did something wild whenever she was upset.

Noah wasn't the one who could help her, by any means. But he could relate to the grief, the not knowing how to handle it. When he'd met her a week ago, he never would've guessed they might have anything in common, but now he thought he'd been wrong.

"Are you feeling any better about moving?" he asked cautiously, as he helped her lie back on the table.

"Nope."

"Is there anything that would make it easier for you?" He regretted the fact that his actions were adding to her problems, even though he'd told himself repeatedly that it wasn't his concern.

She looked at him without moving her head, since he was snipping the thread from her chin at the time. "Don't buy it?"

"If I don't, someone else will."

Katie didn't say anything, and Noah continued to snip and pull threads. The one remaining stitch was stubborn, didn't want to come out. He leaned closer to her face and she closed her eyes.

"All done," he said when he got the last bit out. He held his hand out to help her sit up and was surprised when she actually took it.

She ran the fingers of her left hand over the healing wound. "I know you're right, but it's hard. I'm sure everyone thinks I'm crazy because I'm throwing such a fit over the house."

"I don't think you're crazy. Not for that." He met her gaze and realized he was still holding her hand. He let go of it, then, feeling awkward and unprofessional. "The roof antics, the kayaking and shark-swimming, yes. You're way out there."

She smiled halfheartedly, but the sadness in her eyes was a more powerful message, one she probably didn't even intend.

"It's healing well," Noah said. "Scarring should be minimal. Not that scars seem to deter you much."

Katie shrugged one shoulder. "All part of the deal."

Her tone was nonchalant, matter of fact. Odd that she worried so much about a house, but not about her own body being harmed.

"Do you ever feel fear?" he asked her,

pursuing some urge to understand her better.

She slid off the table to stand on the floor and studied him. Her eyes looked tired, as if she hadn't been sleeping much. "All the time. But that's the whole point. To conquer the fear."

Her words made him uneasy. He busied himself jotting notes on her chart, but he couldn't get the phrase of Katie's out of his mind. *To conquer the fear.* Noah suspected he was living with too much fear these days. Fear that he wouldn't have the first clue about vanquishing. Too bad it wasn't as easy as Katie made it sound.

He pushed the thought away, because it was too uncomfortable.

"Take care of yourself. See if you can stay out of here until it's time to check out your wrist."

"Don't miss me too much when I'm gone." She attempted a light smile, but mostly failed and then walked out the door.

"HAVE YOU NOTICED anything strange going on with Savannah?" Katie asked Lindsey.

They were kneeling outside Lindsey's house, pulling weeds from the flower bed. "Strange how?"

"With Michael. Like maybe they're having problems."

Lindsey turned and looked at Katie thoughtfully. "He's been working a lot lately."

"So she said."

"Enough so that he's missing many of our family things."

"That's convenient. He never used to seem to dislike spending time with us, did he?"

Lindsey shook her head. "He fit in just fine. What prompts all these questions?"

Katie moved closer and looked around to see if anyone could hear. Not only was she going to reveal one of Savannah's secrets, but her own, as well. Zach was mowing the lawn, so the noise from the mower pretty much drowned out her voice anyway.

"I really hate to see Dad sell the house…" she began.

"I've been wanting to talk to you about

that. It's impossible to get any privacy in this family anymore, but why are you having such a hard time with that?"

Katie sighed. She really did hate getting into it, because she knew it was pointless now. The damage was done and the house would soon be Noah's. But she had brought it up knowing Lindsey might pursue the subject. "You probably won't understand since you have a home and a family of your own. You know that feeling you get when you go home? The familiarity, the comfort of just walking in the door and inhaling the way the house smells. The furniture's in the same place, the rugs are worn in the same patterns…"

"It's your home." Lindsey nodded. "I do know what you mean."

"That house over there," she motioned toward their dad's next door, "that's my home. My apartment in St. Louis is nice and it serves its purpose, but it's not the same thing at all."

"I still feel it when I walk in there," Lindsey admitted. "Home and… This will sound strange, but Mom's still there in that house."

Katie looked at her in grateful surprise. "Did Dad tell you how I feel? About my embarrassing emotional rant?"

Lindsey shook her head.

"I'm so scared that losing that house will mean losing half my memories of Mom. I won't be able to *see* her doing things she used to do, like tucking me in at night, painting my fingernails on her bathroom vanity, reading to me on the front steps." Katie sat back with her knees pulled up, hugging them, forgetting the weeding. "Everything was good back then, when Mom was still alive. Those are my happiest memories, and so many of them are tied up in that house. Losing it—" she shook her head "—it's messing with my head."

"Oh, sweetie." Lindsey crawled over to Katie and sat down next to her. "I'm so sorry. I do know what you're saying."

"You do? You're the only one who doesn't think I'm being a whiny baby."

Lindsey grinned. "I know what you mean. I really do. It makes me sad to see the house go, too, but you know what I've figured out? We'll still have the memories. Nothing can take those away from us. You'll still remember Mom and all the good things."

"I'm not so sure about that."

Lindsey put an arm around Katie, leaning her head on Katie's shoulder but not saying anything else. Lindsey's husband, Zach, came around the corner from the front yard at that moment.

"What's going on? Am I the only one toiling away?" He walked up in front of them, hands on his hips, looking down with a smile. "What if I need a little TLC like that?"

Lindsey let go of Katie. "As nasty and sweaty as you are right now? Good luck." Smirking she stood up. "Shower, and we'll talk."

"The sweat proves one of us, at least, has been working."

Lindsey laughed and picked up a hand-

ful of the pulled weeds. She came up behind him and stuck the weeds down the
back of his shirt.

"There's your proof, tyrant. Now do the
backyard. Try not to mow over the pink
kidlets or the elderly woman and her caretaker back there."

Zach shook his head as he emptied the
weeds from his shirt. "You'll pay later."
He disappeared into the garage.

"You two are annoyingly happy," Katie
said lightly.

Lindsey's eyes lit up and her smile bor-
dered on sappiness. She bent down over
the flower bed.

It still blew Katie's mind that Lindsey's
life had changed so much so quickly.
She and Zach had adopted Owen, Zach's
seven-year-old nephew, when Owen's al-
coholic dad left town.

Before Owen's paperwork was even
done, they'd moved ahead on making
Billy, also seven, a permanent part of their
family. He'd been one of Lindsey's charges
as a social worker. She and Zach had fallen

in love with him and had seen how much good Billy and Owen did for each other.

The last piece of their insta-family was Grandma Rundle, a woman Katie—and her sisters, too, for that matter—had once been scared of. They'd all gotten to know a different side of her as she grew older and mellower.

"So before we got off track on the whole house bit, you were talking about Savannah."

Katie stood up to stretch her legs before moving next to the pile of weeds. "I asked her if she and Michael would consider buying Dad's house. This was before Noah made the offer. She blew me off for as long as she could, then finally said it wasn't a good time for them to make any big decisions."

Lindsey rocked back to rest her hips on her heels. "She said that?"

Katie nodded. "Then she cut me off abruptly, in vintage Savannah style."

"Wow. That's saying a lot. I wonder what's going on."

"I don't have any idea, but she wasn't about to tell me more. It was obvious she regretted telling me that much. Maybe you could try to get it out of her?"

"That won't work. Savannah's not one to share her problems. The more personal they are, the more she'll keep them in."

"So what do we do?" The thought of Savannah dealing with marriage problems by herself worried Katie, even if the two of them had never been that close. She loved her sister and couldn't imagine what she was going through, if indeed the problems were serious.

"I guess we'll just be there for her, if and when she needs us. Look for an opening to ask her what's going on, but don't count on her telling. There's not much else we can do."

"We could take her out for a drink. See what she admits," Katie said, grinning wickedly.

"A girls' night out could be a good idea, actually. Let me see if I can make it work here."

"Ball's in your court, Linds. You're the one who specializes in fixing things. I just wander around and count the days till I go back to my job, away from all this traumatic emotional family stuff."

They both laughed. "If only I didn't think you were actually serious. One of these days some guy's going to knock you off your feet and change the way you think about everything."

"Bite your tongue."

"SNEAKING AWAY INTO the night, with your top-secret room measurements?"

Noah turned to see Katie watching him, half smiling, from the backyard of the house he was buying. She sat on the lawn next to a large rose bush with deep pink blossoms. He headed up the driveway toward her. He had to admit that he'd wondered where she was while he'd been measuring the walls of several rooms.

"Are you out here to avoid me?"

As he neared her, he noticed her smile was for show. She seemed mellow, a little melancholy, as she stood up, even though she was trying to put on a happy front. "If I was avoiding you, I'd go up on the roof."

"You'd be pretty safe there. I'm trying to cut back, myself. So what are you up to out here in the grass all alone?"

Katie looked at the rosebush beside her. "Can I ask you a favor?"

"You can always ask."

"Could you… Um, this is sort of dumb, actually."

"Just say it."

"This rosebush on the end was a gift to my mom from me and my sisters. Mother's Day, I think. I wasn't very old, maybe eight."

"That's an old rose. It looks like it's doing well."

"Yeah. I was wondering if you would keep it for me? I mean, not tear it out?"

The thought struck him that she wasn't nearly as shallow as he'd guessed the first time he met her. He'd assumed she was the type who was always in search of a good time. Looking at her now, as she so earnestly asked him to keep her mother's flowers alive, he realized he'd been off-base.

"I'll take care of it for you. *If* you tell me what it needs. Gardening isn't my strength."

Katie looked at the plant uncertainly. "Mine, either. I think Claudia's responsible for keeping it looking so healthy. We can ask her. I don't believe it takes too much work, though. I was just searching for aphids on the leaves, but I can't find any."

"Is that good or bad?"

"Good. Aphids eat the leaves."

"It's a beautiful rose," he said, moving closer to her.

"It's called an Elizabeth Taylor. We thought that was so cool. I have no idea why."

She sat on the grass next to it, leaned forward and sniffed one of the blossoms. Noah sat down next to her, beginning to understand how comforting it must be for her to have something, some physical thing, to remind her of her mother.

When Leah had died, he'd gotten rid of everything that could remind him of her, finding it all much too painful. Now, he realized that might have been a mistake. Maybe clearing things out had slowed down his grieving.

"You can come by and see it anytime."

Katie nodded slowly. "I'm not usually like this," she said, still staring at the nearest rose.

"Like what?"

"Mopey. Sad. So pensive."

"My guess is you're usually out causing trouble, rather than staying home." He was only partly kidding.

"I don't cause trouble. But I do like to have fun. Don't you?"

The question hung in the air like a heavy fog, as he tried to think of an answer.

"I don't know when I last had honest-to-goodness fun. I haven't been much in the mood."

"That's sad. Is it because of what happened to you?"

He didn't answer for a while, focusing

on the sweetness of the rose's scent instead. "I lost someone close to me not too long ago. I'd planned to marry her."

Katie's eyes widened. "Oh, Noah. I'm really sorry. Even though that doesn't help a bit, does it?"

He met her gaze. "You've been through that, too. The 'I'm sorry's' that make you want to scream."

Katie gazed off into space, nodding. "I know people mean well when they say it. And really, I do mean it—I'm sorry you've had to go through something like that. It sucks. But what can a person say?"

"There's nothing."

She nodded. "What happened to her?"

He shook his head, unable to speak.

"How long ago did she die?"

"Almost a year ago."

Katie plucked strands of grass and ripped them, one at a time, before dropping them back on the ground.

"The only reason I mentioned her death is to let you know you're not the only one who may be dealing with some pretty painful things. I can tell you still think about your mom a lot."

"It seems to be emphasized this time at home. Selling the house has forced the issue and I just can't get her off my mind." She ripped another piece of grass into tiny shreds. "I'm really tired of being so down, honestly."

"It doesn't seem like your usual mood."

"What about you? Are you always so down?"

He smiled, noticing how the blue in her eyes seemed to darken with the approaching dusk. "I imagine I'm somewhat more serious than you, even before I met Leah."

"Leah, huh? Was she as uptight as you?"

He tried to smile at the provocative question, but he couldn't pull it off. "Actually, she was a lot like you in many ways. She loved adventure, was spontaneous, full of life."

"Sounds like I'd have liked her."

"You would have."

"What I can't imagine is *you* liking her."

"You can't always help who you care for, I guess."

"I guess. I don't really know much about that. I'm not one to give advice, but you really should find something you like to do for fun. And do it."

He tried to imagine what he might do, but nothing came to mind. "You're probably right. I'll give it some thought."

"This topic is depressing. Want to go out for a shake?"

"A shake?"

"You know, ice cream, sugar-filled flavoring, some milk? Mixed and served with a straw?"

"Empty calories."

"Exactly. Come on, you can drive and I'll treat."

"Do you really want ice cream?"

"A shake. Yes. Really." She looked at him as if he was the odd one. "But if you're too good for the Dairy Delight, it's no big thing."

"Why do you say things like that?"

She shrugged, shooting him an innocent look.

Noah stood and held out a hand to help her. "Not only will I drive us there, but I will prove to you I can embrace my inner child by buying the milkshakes for both of us."

With Noah's help, Katie pulled herself up. "*That* is a fabulous idea." He didn't immediately drop her hand as they walked to his Tahoe.

CHAPTER EIGHT

THE DAIRY DELIGHT was chock-full of people. Even though the sun had set, the temperature was still ninety-two degrees, according to the Lone Oak Bank and Trust sign across the street. As they approached the place, Katie figured about half the town had come out for ice cream tonight.

She opened the door, but Noah pulled her back. "I'm treating, remember? You stay out here, out of the chaos. We can get one of the outdoor tables."

"How could I forget you're treating? Something tells me it's not every day you buy a girl a drink."

"It's not every day I'm harangued into visiting Dairy Delight."

Katie could swear his lips curved into the beginnings of a smile, something she'd rarely seen on him.

"What would you like?" Noah asked.

"I thought we were having milkshakes."

"What flavor?"

"Surprise me."

He looked at her for a moment, then headed inside with a shrug.

As a group of teenagers left one of the outdoor tables, Katie snagged it and sat down. She sat there people watching, trying not to think about the fact that she was out with Noah. It had seemed natural for them to come out for a drink when she'd asked him. But now it was starting to feel too much like a date.

She wasn't against dates at all. Normally. Something about Noah made her leery, though. Possibly the fact that she couldn't use an exciting activity as an excuse for accepting. Half the time, dating was a way to go out and do something fun. Watch a scary movie, take a picnic out on a boat, water ski.

She was with Noah simply because she'd enjoyed talking to him and she was starting to like him.

"One ultra-deluxe surprise milkshake," he said from behind her.

"That's huge. And you acted like such a milkshake novice." Katie used both hands to take the cup from him. "What flavor?"

"You have to guess."

Katie put in her straw and drank. "Easy. Strawberry."

"Not just strawberry. There's banana in there, too. Hope you like it."

"Love it. Next time, I get to surprise you."

"Next time, huh?" Noah sat on the bench beside her and stuck a straw in his milkshake.

"I'm hard to resist. What kind did you get?"

"Berry mix, which is blueberry, raspberry…"

"And blackberry." She laughed.

"You know your milkshake flavors."

"A girl's gotta have expertise in something." She took a drink. "I have to admit, I'm surprised. I'd pegged you for the vanilla type."

"That should teach you."

"I'll consider myself taught. Or something."

"Every time I see you, I notice a new scar. What's this from?" He ran his finger lightly over her left shoulder blade. Her thin-strapped tank revealed most of the mark, but parts of it, she knew, were hidden under the pink cotton.

"That," she said, trying to see it over her shoulder, "was lucky. I wiped out on a surfboard and rammed into some coral with my shoulder."

"That's lucky, is it?"

"It beat ramming my head against it and ending up with a concussion or worse."

He took several sips of his shake, then nodded. "I guess if you look at it that way."

"That way is much better than worrying about what could've happened."

"So tell me," Noah said, "when did you start with all the daredevil stunts?" He seemed a little uneasy, as if it was a strain to make idle conversation.

"When I was born."

He raised his eyebrows doubtfully.

"Really. My mom used to tell stories about me climbing on top of the refrigerator before I was three years old."

"The poor woman."

"Yeah. I probably put her through a lot."

"Don't we all?"

"You? No way."

"I was nothing like you, I'm sure."

"I didn't start the really fun stuff until after my mom died."

"What kind of 'stuff'?" he asked. He looked as if he might not really want to know. "The climbing up on the roof?"

"I guess that was when I first made it up there." She nodded, impressed he'd picked up on that. "As for sports, I started out easy. Snowboarding, skiing, skateboarding. A couple years later, I started whitewater rafting."

"Lots of rapids around these parts."

"A sarcastic side," Katie said, studying him in surprise. "I like." She rotated her cup on the table. "I went to Colorado with a friend's family."

"How old were you?"

"Probably sixteen."

He frowned. "Anything else you tried before starting at the magazine?"

"Hang-gliding. Bungee jumping. My dad nearly had a stroke when he found out about that one. Storm chasing."

Noah shook his head slowly, looking puzzled. The kidding mood that had lasted for all of five seconds was gone. "I don't get it. Why would you want to risk your life on a regular basis?"

Katie stared at him, sipping her shake. Now she put it down. "Don't tell me volunteering in Africa was a risk-free endeavor." She sensed he was really bothered by her tendency toward adventure, but she couldn't figure out why.

"That was different. The purpose wasn't to risk my life, it was to accomplish something."

"Who's to say I'm not accomplishing something when I'm flying off the side of a mountain?"

"And what would that be?"

"Living."

Katie slid her shake to the side and leaned her elbows on the table, clenching her fists together. "I learned long ago, you never know what might happen tomorrow."

"Why does living have to involve physical risk?"

"That's what I like to do. I like to feel the fear. Better yet, I like to overcome that fear."

He tossed his shake—which he'd barely started—into a nearby trash barrel. "What about the people who care about you? Your family? Do you ever think how much you worry them? What would happen to them if you got yourself killed?"

There was anger in his words and Katie couldn't for the life of her see why he was mad at her. Hadn't they just been having a semi-philosophical conversation? This felt personal.

"Should I live my life in a safe little box, maybe in a sleepy small town like Lone Oak, just to keep my family happy?"

"Life here doesn't have to be dull."

"You've already had your fun. You went out and did what you wanted to in Africa and wherever else your noble cause took you. Now you're ready to settle down and hide. Some of us are still into living life to the fullest."

"Like I said, my dangerous work had a purpose."

"I suppose your family worried less, since you were saving lives and all."

Noah ran his hand over the stubble on his face. His eyes were dull with fatigue, but that wasn't Katie's fault. He was the one who'd started attacking her lifestyle.

"Why do you act as if the way I live will affect *you,* anyway? It has nothing to do with you."

His jaw tensed and he looked away. "You're absolutely right. We should get going."

Katie stood. "We should." She stalked off to his Tahoe and waited for him to unlock her door.

They rode the short distance back to the

Salingers' house in silence. Katie sat wondering what had just happened. When he pulled into her dad's driveway, she wasted no time. "Thanks for the shake."

She got out and shut the door before Noah could say a word.

SHE RATTLED HIM, plain and simple. And Noah didn't know if he was angry primarily at himself or primarily at Katie. Himself, because he'd let her see how bothered he could be if he thought about what she did for a living. Or for fun. Katie, because she lived on the edge in a way that scared him to death, made him worry. For her, for her family, for anyone who cared about her.

Why should he care? He wasn't part of her life. There might be a slight attraction to her, but that meant nothing. It was just that he understood the grief she lived with and he knew how hard it was. Wanted to help her through it.

But he sure couldn't afford to get involved with someone like Katie again. Not romantically. Love with an adventurous soul wasn't for the faint of heart. He'd learned that lesson far too well.

It didn't matter what he felt in his heart. This time, he was listening to his head, and his head said stay away.

"STAND BACK, DAD. Let me do this part," Noah said. He fought with the crank on the lift to lower the two-year-old boat into the water.

"I've let you do everything other than hold the door open. What's with you? You're treating me like some delicate woman."

"You don't need to do the heavy stuff. Once we get the boat in the water, you can take over."

His father glared at him and Noah knew he'd offended him. Tough. It was better than having him strain a muscle or over-work his heart—or worse.

"If we're going to fish together, you better set aside the dictatorship. You forget who taught you to do all this," Ivan said grumpily.

"I remember perfectly well. That's why

I invited you. *One* of the reasons," Noah added quickly.

This experiment had two purposes. First, he was at a loss when it came to the subject of things to do for fun, as Katie had suggested. He wouldn't normally follow advice from such a person, but this made sense. He had nothing in his life, right now, except work, reading up on research, taking care of his parents and preparing to move into his own home. Oh, and jogging. He did enjoy that, to an extent, but he wouldn't exactly call it fun. So why not try fishing. He'd done it lots when he was growing up.

The second reason for taking his dad on this outing was that getting *him* back into fishing might slow him down a little, get him to relax. Lower his blood pressure, if it needed to come down. Noah actually didn't know much about the fine points of his dad's health, because his dad never shared such information. Most likely so that Noah wouldn't intervene.

If they could enjoy some time together out on the water, it'd be a bonus.

The boat touched the surface of the water and Noah kept on turning the crank until it completely cleared the platform.

"You going to let me get in now?" his dad asked.

Noah stifled a chuckle. "Just be careful. Take it slowly."

"Yes, Mama," his dad said this with another glare.

So maybe enjoying some time together out on the water wasn't going to happen, after all.

The older man climbed in and pulled his keys out of his pocket.

"Think it'll start?" Noah asked.

"Yes, I do. It's in perfect condition."

Noah waited, knowing his dad hadn't been out in it since the summer he'd bought it. It started right up, though. The noise of the motor echoed off the walls of the small boathouse.

"Meet you at the dock," Noah hollered.

He shut the garage door and headed outside through the regular door.

His dad guided the boat up to the dock and Noah climbed in.

"Let's see how this thing moves," his father said.

"I have no doubt it can move."

They motored along at a good pace and Noah tried to pick out familiar landmarks on the shore. It'd been years since he'd been on the river—since he was in high school, in fact, and now nothing looked the same. Of course, then he'd just had a canoe.

"Why don't you fish more often?" he asked his father.

"Time, mostly. It gets away from you."

"I don't know how you've been handling the workload at the clinic, to be honest."

"Long hours. A patient wife."

"I've been thinking," Noah began, though he hadn't planned to have this conversation just yet. "Maybe it'd be wise for us to look at bringing a third doctor on board."

There was no response to this, and Noah wasn't sure he'd heard. Then his father looked at him, straight on.

"You've got lots of plans, don't you?"

"What's that supposed to mean? All I'm getting at is, we could use some help."

"*You're* my help. We're doing fine."

"We're doing fine, if an hour wait is acceptable for our patients."

"That's the worst-case scenario, and you know it."

"We could build the practice to be the best in the area, Dad."

"We're the only practice in town."

"You've been resting on that for too long. People won't hesitate to drive ten miles down the road to see a Layton doctor."

"They will if they know anything about him. He's a quack. Acupuncture, Chinese herbs… I don't even know what all he's passing off as medical care over there."

Noah tapped his fingers on the edge of the boat, trying to summon extra patience. "You might be surprised how popular alternative health care is becoming. We could stand to open our minds a bit on the subject."

His dad gave him a horrified grunt. "What are they teaching these days at med school?"

"Same things they were teaching in your day, Dad." This wasn't the time to argue medical philosophy. "Back to our practice, though. We're booked. Every day."

"And I'm thankful for it."

The discussion was going nowhere. Plus, it was defeating the whole purpose of being out on the water. They hadn't brought any fishing gear today. This was just to see how the boat did after two years off—a test run of sorts.

"This isn't the end of our discussion," Noah said. "We need to do something so you won't have to spend ten hours a day at the office."

"Whatever you're trying to pull, you can stop anytime. Try to remember, I did just fine all those years you were away."

"But you're older now."

"You're worse than your mother. Where did you learn to nag?"

Noah shook his head and faced the water, making a mental note that in order to relax, he was probably going to have to fish alone.

CHAPTER NINE

KATIE WATCHED THE movers roll the last load of boxes, stacked three high, out to the truck.

It was done. The house was empty.

Her footsteps echoed as she walked from room to room over the bare floors. Her dad and Claudia were at the new place already, unpacking things delivered in the first truckload and waiting to tell the movers where to put the rest of their stuff once it arrived. Katie was glad, now, that she'd volunteered for this end of the job. She couldn't do much in the way of lifting and loading with her arm in a cast, so she'd just directed the movers when they needed instructions. Watched them empty out her home of twenty-some years and turn it into a "pile of wood and bricks," as Savannah had described it.

Katie took the stairs up to the top floor, her limbs aching with bone-deep emotional fatigue. She couldn't bring herself to walk out the door just yet.

She went directly to the master bedroom and walked across it to a window seat in the dormer.

This had been one of her favorite places when she'd been young. She'd ask her mom to read to her, and then lead her here. Back then, there'd been overstuffed pillows lining the seat, but now nothing softened it. There was only a wooden bench with thinly cushioned upholstery on the surface. Nothing like the special place she'd shared with her mom so long ago.

Perhaps she was torturing herself, trying to hoard as many memories as she could. Hoping to file them away, somehow, so she wouldn't lose them.

She made a quick check through all the upstairs rooms, to make certain they hadn't left anything behind. Her closet door was open now and she smiled through her tears at the organizer her mom had installed in an effort to help Katie be neater. The endeavor had been a failure and the family had joked about Katie's inability to keep her room clean ever since.

As she headed for the stairs again, she held on to her heart necklace, wishing it could offer the same comfort that holding her mother's hand always had.

"Get over it," she told herself when she got to the main floor. "It's just a building." She sat on the steps, lost in her thoughts, having no success whatsoever in following her own advice.

Finally, she stood slowly, grabbed her purse and a soft drink from the kitchen counter, and headed out the front door without looking back. She could barely see where she was going through her tears.

KATIE PULLED HER JEEP up along the curb on the far side of the moving truck and hopped out after composing herself somewhat. If she had her way, she'd sit here in the street forever and avoid going inside. The moving men already had the back of the truck open and were starting to unload it, but her dad and stepmom were nowhere in sight.

She walked slowly up the driveway, giving the movers a hard time as she went. Finally she reached the front door of the square, characterless house, which was propped open. Up until now, she'd avoided entering the place. Her dad had tried several times to get her to go with them to see it, but she hadn't been able to work up the interest. She'd held on to her denial for as long as she could.

After composing herself, she stepped over the threshold. Already, the couch was placed along one of the walls in the living room. The couch that had been in *her* home for years. It didn't fit here at all. It no longer felt comfortable or wholly familiar.

"Hello?" she called. It echoed through the half-empty rooms.

"Hey, honey. There you are." Her dad came out from the kitchen. "Come on in here. We're just unpacking the necessities."

She went to the doorway of the kitchen. It was modern, sparkling clean, full of white cabinets and stainless-steel appliances. The exact opposite of the traditional coziness of her old home. She wondered if they had chosen this on purpose.

"I'm going to look around," she said, trying her best to ignore the feeling of being totally lost.

Everything was on one floor, which would be good for her dad's heart. She continued through the living room to a hallway. There were three doorways close to each other, two on one side and the other across the hall.

She poked her head into the first one and found it nearly full with the first truckload of furniture. Her dad's office. The next room was clearly the master suite, even though there was no furniture in it so far, only a pile of boxes against one wall.

Finally, she walked into the third room. She knew instantly this one was supposed to be hers; there was her own bed in the corner.

Just as quickly, she knew she could never stay here, would never call this place home. It wasn't that it was a bad room, it was just…not hers. Instead of having the feeling of belonging, she felt as if she were walking into a dorm room that had served its purpose for dozens of other people. As if putting anything on the walls would be pointless.

Katie turned away, a sharp pain shooting through her head.

No way could she stay here.

She walked directly out the front door and back to her Jeep. She'd planned to stay in Lone Oak for her last three weeks of enforced healing time, but not anymore. She'd needed comfort and now that was gone.

She drove to Savannah's house, hoping they'd finished the basement as they'd planned to do a few months ago and had put a bed down there. And if they hadn't, cement floors and a cot would be just fine for the next couple of nights until she headed back to St. Louis.

She rang Savannah's doorbell. Her brother-in-law Michael opened the door.

"Katie." He held out his arms and she hugged him. "How's my favorite kid sister?"

"Still your only kid sister." She kissed his cheek, then looked him over closely for any signs of strain. She would have to have been blind to miss the tension in his face, the way his mouth fell into a frown of sad resignation.

"Have you eaten?" he asked. "We just sat down to dinner."

"I didn't mean to interrupt."

"Burgers. We've got plenty. Come on in."

Katie followed him into the kitchen.

"Aunt Katie!"

"What are you doing here? I thought you'd still be helping with the move." Savannah got up and took an extra plate from the cupboard.

"Thanks. Sorry to barge in at dinnertime. I didn't even realize what time it was."

"So are they all done with the big stuff?" Savannah asked.

Katie filled her plate. "They're just unloading the second truckload. Got a ways to go."

"And you took off?"

"Hey, I lasted longer than you did." Savannah had left after lunch, to take the kids to swimming lessons. "Actually, I wasn't doing anyone much good. Then I saw the new house."

"And... What'd you think?"

"It's okay, I guess." She took a bite of her burger and chewed, glancing at the kids and trying to decide how much to say. "I don't think I can stay there. I was wondering if your basement was in shape enough for me to stay down there."

"It's finished," Savannah said. "It's almost a full apartment. Only thing it lacks is a kitchen. What do you think, Michael?"

He didn't even look at his wife. "Why ask me? You're the one in charge of everything around here."

O-kay. If that wasn't indicative of a deeper problem, Katie didn't know what was. The kids were quiet, pretending to be engrossed by their food.

Savannah shot him a killer look, then turned her attention back to Katie. "You're welcome to stay down there for as long as you need to."

"Thanks," Katie said, extremely concerned by the bad vibes snapping between Savannah and her husband. "It'll only be for a couple nights, until I can get organized. I'm going to head back to St. Louis."

"Thought you'd planned on staying until your medical leave was over."

"I made those plans before I knew we'd be leaving the old house."

"Dad will be upset if you don't stay with them," Savannah said.

Katie finished a mouthful of chips and shrugged. "He knows how I feel."

"Maybe you should try to get over it," Savannah said.

"I *am* trying. I feel awful being upset about this. It's a house—just a house. It makes no sense."

"I couldn't have said it better myself," Savannah said, amused.

"Anyways, leave me and my issues alone," Katie said halfheartedly, not really upset. "I'll go back over after a while to see if I can help with something, and I'll tell them I'm going to crash here."

"I'll come with you. Maybe we can present it as a sisterly bonding thing. You know, a chance for us to stay up late, talking about girl stuff."

"Yeah, except Dad knows better. You and I don't bond and we don't talk about girlie things."

"Good point. So we'll just tell him you hate the house."

"Sounds like a fun conversation to have."

"You know, you could stay a little longer than two nights."

Katie looked carefully at her sister. If she didn't know better, she'd almost think Savannah wanted her hanging around. She glanced at Michael again, but he was ignoring them, reading the newspaper and finishing his dinner.

"I...might," Katie said cautiously. "If you think I should."

Of course, Savannah admitted to nothing.

KATIE HAD SPENT enough time in hotels across the country that one more bed shouldn't have bothered her. And in fact, last night it hadn't. After an emotionally draining day spent moving her dad and then explaining to him that she couldn't stay in his new house and was heading back to St. Louis early, she'd collapsed in Savannah's basement and fallen into an exhausted dreamless sleep. Tonight, however, that wasn't happening.

Katie sat up in bed and stuck her legs over the side. Savannah's guest bed was comfortable—with a fluffy, lightweight down comforter and soft clean sheets—but physical comfort wasn't going to quell her restlessness now. She jumped up, switched on the ancient lamp on the nightstand and surveyed the room, not sure what she was looking for. It was a hodge-podge of mis-matched furniture—an old white dresser, a recliner, an end table, a small dining set—but somehow it all came together to be homey, cozy. And cool. Katie shivered from the combination of central air conditioning and an insulated basement. Then she started pacing.

She allowed that energy to carry her up the stairs without much thought then let herself out onto the back patio, closing the door silently.

The sticky night was full of sounds, calming ones. The chirp of crickets. The harmonized whirr of the neighbors' air conditioners. A light wind rustling the leaves in the trees. She inhaled the humid air, thinking if she breathed in enough of it, the peace of the evening might fill her.

The moon was bright, inviting her to stray from the safety of the backyard. She had no plans when she started walking barefoot down the driveway, onto the side-walk. She didn't worry about the fact she was wearing only her pajamas—a thin-

strapped tank and baggy cotton pants—
since no one in this sleepy town was
stirring anyway. Didn't worry where she
was heading, either, and soon found herself three blocks from Savannah's.

Right smack in front of the home they'd
just moved her dad and stepmom out of.

The entire main floor was brightly
lit. Katie walked a few steps farther, toward the driveway, and saw Noah's Tahoe
pulled up in front of the garage. An in-
explicable relief went through her at the
sight, as if she'd wanted to see him. She
hadn't, not consciously. They hadn't spoken since they'd left the Dairy Delight the
other night on less-than-friendly terms.

She walked up to the front door, craning
her neck to try to get a glimpse of Noah,
but the living room—in the front of the
house—appeared to be unoccupied. She
rang the doorbell and smiled sadly at the
familiarity of the sound.

She heard footsteps approaching, then

Noah opened the door. He wore cutoff sweats, an ancient paint-spattered Gumby T-shirt and a frown.

CHAPTER TEN

"WHAT ARE YOU doing here?" Noah asked, making no motion to invite her inside.

"I could ask you the same thing. Don't you have to work tomorrow?"

He nodded. "I want to get the painting done before I move in this weekend. It's easier when there's no furniture."

"What are you painting? Are you changing the colors?" She looked beyond him anxiously.

Noah thought for a moment, realizing he wasn't likely to get rid of Katie too easily. In spite of his determination to stay away from her, he found he couldn't help feeling sympathy now. Clearly, she was still having trouble letting go of the house. Sympathy and...something else. Something better left unexplored.

The least he could do was let her in and

see if that helped her to understand that it was no longer her family's home.

"Yes, I'm changing the colors. I think the living room looks good, but it's definitely different." Noah casually rested his hand on her waist as they moved toward the room, then pulled it away when he realized what he'd done and thought about how natural it had felt. "Remember that in a few weeks, you won't know the difference. You won't be able to tell when I so much as plant a new tree in front, because you'll be miles away, caught up in your next adrenaline rush."

"Tomorrow, actually."

"Tomorrow what?"

"I'm going back to St. Louis."

"What for?" A part of him—the part that had reached out and touched her just a minute ago—was sorry to hear she was leaving.

"That's where I live, remember? This is no longer my home, in any sense of the word."

"I thought you were staying here while you couldn't work."

"I was going to. Until I went into my dad's new house yesterday. I couldn't stand it. It's depressing. It just emphasizes the fact that that's not where we belong. That our home is gone. Yeah, this looks like a different place," she said, paying attention to the walls at last. "Brown, huh? Very...masculine. Something my mother would never have chosen."

"Desert khaki," he corrected her. "It's darker than I expected, but I like it. I'm sorry it makes you sad though." He found he meant it.

Katie turned in circles, taking it in.

"I'm hopelessly hung up on how it was, you know." She blew out the air from her lungs. "I never really thought about it, but we've kept everything the same ever since she died. Even when we repainted, we bought the same colors my mom had chosen. We're a sick bunch, huh?"

He'd had the exact same thought about himself in the past, when he couldn't let go of the crushing sadness of losing Leah. He'd much rather try to help Katie through her grief than work through his own, though.

Regardless of his promise to himself to keep his distance from Katie, he couldn't be harsh or mean or cruel when she showed him how upset she still was. All he could do was fight the urge to pull her into his arms—an urge that was building instead of diminishing.

"You're not sick," he said. "People handle their losses in different ways. Who's to say what's the right way to do it?"

Katie met his gaze. "Yeah. True." She turned back toward the walls. "But it's been long enough. I need to let go."

"Something tells me we never really let go of our mothers, whether they're alive or not." He moved so he could see her face in profile and realized there was moisture in her eyes.

"Hey," Noah said, touching her cheek with his knuckles.

She turned her head to his and smiled

sadly. "I swear I didn't come over here to cry on your shoulder."

"Yes, that reminds me. Why *did* you come over here?"

"I honestly don't know." She faced him fully now. "I couldn't sleep. I went outside and it was so nice out there, so I started walking. This is where I ended up."

"In your—" Noah let his gaze move over her "—pajamas."

Longing ignited in him as he noticed the rosy flush on her cheeks. He wanted to touch her, pull her close to him, kiss away her troubles.

And that was completely inappropriate. She'd come here for comfort, to process a loss. Whether she'd *meant* to show up or not, she was drawn here because she was upset. If she knew the thought that had just coursed through Noah's mind she'd no doubt slap him.

Or maybe she wouldn't. The way she looked up at him at that moment made his breath catch in his throat. He looked away, afraid he was a moment away, at most, from doing something stupid.

"If you give me five minutes to finish washing out brushes, I'll give you a ride home," he told her, heading to the kitchen and away from temptation.

"You don't need to do that." She followed him. "I'm sorry to show up here, uninvited. At this hour."

"Nights are harder, aren't they?"

She looked at him sharply, then nodded. "Darkness seems to affect everything, make things more difficult."

She joined him at the sink, taking one of the paint-soaked brushes from the tray and holding it under running water. Their elbows were side by side, brushing together every so often, and Noah became completely focused on the fleeting contact.

As they stood there in silence, rinsing out paint, he fought a war with himself. He wanted to kiss her, but he'd already told himself getting any closer to her would be a giant mistake. Because no matter how calm and rational she seemed at this moment, she was still an impulsive risk taker, an enjoy-life-at-all-costs person. And he couldn't live with that.

He finished the brush he was working on and stepped away from Katie, away from the sink. Then he picked up the thin plastic tarp he'd used in the living room, wadded it into a ball and shoved it into a large trash bag.

Time to get out of here. He'd come far too close to doing something he shouldn't. Tomorrow she'd be gone, and while he was a little sorry to hear the news, at least he'd escape without succumbing to the temptation of getting any closer.

Katie finished the last brush and set it down to dry.

"Let's go," Noah said.

"Go where?"

"I'll take you home. It's late."

She glanced at the clock on the stove. "I told you I can get myself home. Do you want me to throw the brushes in a plastic bag for you to take with you?"

"No. I'll need them tomorrow."

"You're painting more?"

"Tomorrow's the kitchen. I hope to get the whole main floor repainted before the weekend."

He could tell when she noticed the bare kitchen walls for the first time. He'd spent several hours stripping the wallpaper. She stood there, seeming to absorb all the changes. Instead of the concern she'd shown when she'd first seen the living room, she nodded. "I guess it probably needs it, huh?"

Katie noticed the way Noah was staring at her… again. As if he was feeling the same thing she was feeling. She wanted to kiss him, wanted to find out how it felt to have his arms wrapped around her. She'd thought he might kiss her when he'd noticed she was wearing her pajamas but then he'd backed away.

He went into the other room, now, and she heard him lock the front door and turn off the lights.

"Ready?" Noah asked as he returned. He opened the back door and held it for her.

As she passed by him, she caught his scent, which should've been unappealing. He'd worked the entire day and then spent the night painting. But all she smelled was man and paint. It seemed so personal. Drew her to him, made her want to get even closer and bury her face in his chest. Just the scent did odd, tingly things to her insides.

She walked to the passenger door of the Tahoe and was about to open it when Noah grabbed the handle first. Katie turned to look at him, smiling.

"Are you always such a gentleman?"

He lowered his eyes to her lips and Katie felt the tingling again.

"Are you always such a..." He frowned. "Forget I said anything."

"Such a what?" she asked. "That could end up being either good or bad. What were you going to say?"

He tried to turn away, but Katie stepped toward him now and touched his arm. "Noah." They were less than a foot apart and she moved closer still, making eye contact inescapable. He stopped trying to get away and stared into her eyes. "Remember that conversation we had about finding time for fun?"

"Yeah." The word sounded husky.

"Now would be a good time to try it."

"You think so?"

They moved together until their bodies were touching. Instead of waiting for Noah, Katie stretched upward and kissed him. At the first touch, she felt herself falling, floating, just like when she stepped out of an airplane. But along with that usual rush came a special electric thrill that shot deep inside her.

Noah's arms closed around her, his hands running over her back.

"See?" she said. "Fun is good."

He groaned something akin to agreement, then deepened the kiss. Her entire being was focused on the tantalizing feel of his lips on hers.

Whoa. This was dangerous ground.

Katie pulled away from his kiss just

enough for him to open his eyes questioningly.

"We're moving from fun to dangerous in record time," she said lightly, breathing unevenly.

"You could be right." He nuzzled her hair, kissed the sensitive spot by her ear.

"I'm usually right," she said, grinning. "I was right about the fun thing."

"Not really." His lips were still near her ear. She shivered.

"Not really?" It was hard to focus on the conversation. "Not fun?"

Noah shook his head. "*Fun* is such a mundane word. This is more…*intoxicating.*"

Katie chuckled. "That's definitely a first."

"What?"

"I've never had a guy say kissing me is intoxicating."

"Then your previous guys have been lacking in imagination."

"More likely they've been lacking in vocabulary. I've never kissed a doctor be-

fore." She ran her finger over the rough
stubble on his cheek, and then across his
lips. Noah kissed the tip.

"I guess you've been missing out."

"Something like that." Her voice
sounded odd to her—breathless. "You realize you have patients to see in how many
hours?"

He nodded and leaned in to brush his
lips across hers one last time. "Let's get
you home."

He held Katie's hand as she climbed into
his SUV, then shut her door and walked
around to the driver's side. Before climbing in, he inhaled deeply, wondering how
long it was going to take his head to clear.

They were silent on the drive, save for
Katie's brief directions to Savannah's
house. He pulled into the driveway just
far enough to get off the street, not wanting to draw attention to their arrival. He
felt like a kid sneaking his girl home after
curfew.

Before he could think any more about
how twisted that was, Katie leaned over

and pressed her lips to his once again. Just when he'd managed to get his pulse back down into the normal range.

"You know what?" she whispered. "I'm starting to think serious is exciting."

He had no idea what to say to that and thankfully didn't have to as she hopped out.

"Night," she said before shutting the door.

He watched her make her way up the driveway, keeping his eyes on her until she disappeared around the corner of the house.

He sat for a moment longer, closing his eyes and trying to regain control of himself. Between fatigue and excitement, his head felt full of...fuzz.

So much for his big doctor's vocabulary.

He shook his head as he backed out and headed to his parents' place, where he'd be sleeping for a few more nights. He tried not to let his mind wander to kissing Katie. Tried but failed.

He crept into his parents' dark house

and went directly to his bedroom, not turning on a light until he'd closed his door.

He took off his shoes and sat on the bed, still warmed by the rush contact with Katie had given him.

The rush.

He looked at his nightstand, contemplating the stack of back issues of *Rush* magazine that he'd found at the office. The top one was opened to another eyewitness article by Katie. The primary photo was of her and several others white-water rafting. It didn't take a great imagination to picture her knocking her head on one of the huge boulders, becoming unconscious and being washed down the river.

His warm buzz vanished and the too-familiar panic set in. The pain in his neck overwhelmed him, as if he'd just suffered whiplash. Sweat beaded on his forehead.

Leah had gone rafting, too. He'd been chilled when she'd told him all about it, but his reaction now was stronger. He knew he'd been gun-shy since her death.

Knew he couldn't handle another woman remotely like Leah.

So what on earth was he doing?

Noah had kissed plenty of women before. He'd been serious with only a few, but even in med school he'd made time for dates here and there. He knew with absolute certainty that kissing Katie was on the explosive cardiac-arrest end of the spectrum. He'd never experienced *anything* like that before, not even with Leah.

That realization frightened him like a mile-wide tornado couldn't.

KATIE LET HERSELF into Savannah's house. Thanks to her impromptu tryst with Noah, she was now full of an entirely different kind of restless energy than she'd had when she left the house. And she was even further from being able to sleep.

She went through the kitchen, grabbing a bottle of water from the fridge, and into the living room, hoping to raid Savannah's bookshelf, which was full of paperbacks. Just as she was about to flip on the lamp, she realized someone was on the couch.

Instantly, she recognized Savannah's hair falling over the end of it, thanks to the moonlight that was shining in.

Her sister didn't stir. Katie backed out of the room, feeling as if she'd walked in on a big secret. Why wasn't Savannah sleeping with Michael in their room?

She knew, at once, that the vibes she'd picked up between the two of them at dinner were not just the signs of a single bad day. Katie closed her eyes and leaned against the doorjamb. If Savannah and Michael were no longer sharing a bed, things were serious. This looked like a major problem. Katie couldn't wrap her brain around it.

Michael was one of the most laid-back, caring, gentle people she knew. It took a lot to get to him. Had he kicked Savannah out of their bed or was she on the couch by choice? Was it just for tonight or did she sleep there all the time? Either way, it didn't look good for them.

Katie slowly headed down the stairs, concerned about her sister, worried about

Logan and Allie, and, yes, worried about the brother-in-law she'd grown to love.

The darker side of love could tear people apart and she hoped that wasn't about to happen here.

Remembering Savannah's offer that Katie could stay as long as she wanted to, she began to rethink her plans to leave in the morning. Maybe she should stick around and find out if her sister was okay. There was nothing she could do herself to help their marriage, but if there was trouble, at least she could be there for Savannah.

CHAPTER ELEVEN

"I THOUGHT YOU were leaving town," Noah said when he opened his door the next evening. After a day given over to hardcore regret for kissing her, Katie wasn't the person Noah most wanted to see. Even if she did look extremely pretty with her hair pulled back and stray tendrils framing her face.

"That's not the best way to greet someone who's volunteering to help you paint," Katie said. "And…I brought provisions." She held up two tall paper cups.

"You make it hard for a man to say no." He backed up so that she could come inside and then shut the door. "Aren't you supposed to be back in St. Louis?"

"Turns out my sister wanted me to stay longer."

Noah nodded, barely registering what she said. She walked into the kitchen and he followed her, trying to decide if he should ask her to leave. The fact was, he really needed the help she was offering. But after last night, he also knew he needed to keep sufficient distance to avoid touching her, purposely or otherwise.

"You're sure you wouldn't rather spend your time with your sister?" he asked.

A frown formed on Katie's lips. "Yeah, I'm sure. Plus, I thought maybe if I actually helped you transform this place, it'd be easier for me to let go of it. And of course there's the benefit to you that you won't be here until after midnight again."

"Of course. Shakes?" he asked, gesturing toward the cups. She knew his weak points. But so far, she'd kept it pretty impersonal, with no sign of trying to start something more intimate again.

"Of course." She put down her purse, then peeled off the straw wrappers and stuck one in each cup. "Strawberry marshmallow or chocolate-covered cherry. Which do you want?"

"Do I get to try both?"

She shrugged and held up one cup for him. "You don't like to just jump, do you?"

He shook his head. "I prefer to know all my options and weigh them carefully before deciding." She held the drink closer to him and he took a sip. "Strawberry marshmallow?"

She nodded.

"Not bad."

Then she held the other up and he tried it. He swallowed and thought for a moment, comparing the tastes. "I'll take B. Chocolate-covered cherry. Both are excellent options, though."

"Glad you approve."

She handed him the milkshake and took a long sip of her own. Then she looked at the kitchen walls, which he'd barely started painting. He had, however, taped all the cabinets and molding.

"Green?"

"Not green." He groped around for the paint sample, then held it up. "Misty sage."

She squinted at the small patch of wall

that already had the new color on it. "Ah, yes. I see it now. Misty sage all the way."

"I only have one paint tray," he said. "But I do have an extra roller." He took another long drink of his shake, then rummaged in a bag from the hardware store and dug out a second roller.

"Lucky for me." She held out her hand.

"You're serious about helping?" he asked.

"I didn't wear old ratty clothing for nothing." Her shorts were faded cutoffs and her bright blue T had lavender splatters on it.

"And here I thought you were just trying to impress me."

The look she gave him was flirty and mischievous, and Noah reminded himself he needed to be careful. Had to watch what he said, because he didn't have any intention of initiating anything here.

"Where do you want me to start?" she asked, to his relief.

"The big wall." He indicated the wall opposite the one he was working on. Call him a coward, but the farther away he stayed, the better. One whiff of her feminine scent and he'd begin to think about those alluring lips...

Okay, he knew it was a terrible idea for him to accept her help, but this room was a big job and he needed to get more sleep than he'd ended up with last night. He'd barely made it through the day today. He would ignore his attraction to her and just worry about getting the room painted.

Yeah. So he was a sucker. At least he'd try to be a strong one.

They worked in silence for several minutes, the only sound the *squish squish* of their rollers going up and down on the walls. Noah focused on the surface in front of him, making sure every last speck of it was covered with green paint. He attempted not to notice the shapely length of Katie's legs, which was a challenge because of the denim shorts that revealed so much of them. He glanced behind him again and took in how cute she looked in her splattered T-shirt, one arm still in a cast. He turned back and forced out thoughts that would only get him into trouble.

"This color's nice," Katie said, after she'd covered most of her wall. "My mom would've liked it, too. She loved color. That's why none of the rooms were white."

Noah wasn't sure how to respond to this, so he didn't. He poured more paint into the tray, and as Katie walked over to redrench her roller she glanced down at him.

"Yes, I know I'm hung up on my mom."

"I didn't say anything."

"You gave me a look. I'm sorry. I'll try to shut up about her."

"You don't need to do that. Do whatever helps."

"I like to talk about her. The rest of my family would rather avoid the subject most of the time."

As for Noah, he would rather think about anything other than Leah. Avoidance could do wonders. "Has anyone ever told you you're an odd duck?"

"A few times. Usually my sisters. They don't like getting emotional."

"Do you?"

She shrugged, rolling more paint over the wall. "I wouldn't say I like it, but it's part of living, you know?"

"You and this 'living' thing." He tried to make the words light, but failed. "I'm not sure I understand it."

She stood back to survey her work and, apparently satisfied she hadn't missed any spots, laid the roller across the tray and headed for her shake and a paintbrush to use on the corners. He turned back to his painting.

"It's something you figure out when someone dies," she said, and he had to remind himself that she didn't know much about his loss. Probably didn't remember he'd told her the woman he'd been engaged to had died. "Or at least I did. You think you've got unlimited time to do everything, feel everything, say everything. But you don't, necessarily. My mom didn't."

He squeezed his eyes shut, his back still

toward her, caught completely off guard by the pain her words triggered.

He heard her sip her shake, set it down and then walk closer to him. He sucked in air and tried to compose himself.

"When my mom died, I was so struck by that notion. So worried about what she'd never gotten to do in her life. She always said she wanted to learn to ice-skate. Every time we saw ice-skating on TV, she'd wonder how it felt to speed over the ice so fast. She thought maybe it was like flying, but she never once got to try."

Her eyes teared up and Noah looked around for a tissue, but all he had was a roll of paper towels. He swallowed hard on the emotion that was rising in his throat.

"During the funeral, that was all I could think about. She'd never get to ice-skate." Katie tried to laugh, but it came out sounding more like a sob.

Noah touched her arm, thinking her tears would start spilling over any moment. But when she met his gaze, she smiled sadly. He could still feel her sorrow and it made his chest ache.

She picked up the paint can and went back to her side of the room to finish the narrow edges.

"The thing is, I learned. I never assume anything about the future, because who knows what will happen."

Noah nodded, understanding all too well what she meant. "So that's where all this talk about living comes from." He hoped she didn't notice the slight quaver in his voice.

"I don't know if she died with regrets, but I don't want to. I want to jam pack everything in, every day."

Noah started on a new wall.

He did get her, at least in theory. What they differed over was *how* to live life to the fullest. "Has it ever occurred to you that there are other ways of living besides tempting serious injury?" He said this before he'd thought it through.

"Like what? What do *you* consider living, oh, wise master?"

He sighed. "We're probably better off not going down that road again."

"Yep. We'll never agree, until you decide that maybe jumping out of a plane is cool."

He thought he detected a note of kidding in her voice, but he shuddered all the same.

"But without arguing, what do you like to do? Do you just work and run?"

He hated to admit how close to the truth that was. "I'm going to start fishing."

"That's a step in the right direction, I guess."

"Have *you* ever gone fishing?"

"No. I think it'd make me batty. Sitting still and being quiet?"

He nodded, knowing she was probably right, thinking that this was yet another way in which they were incompatible.

"But it's good you're doing something for fun."

The very word *fun* took him right back to the night before, to the embarrassment he felt now. The regret.

Neither of them spoke for quite some

time. Noah was determined to finish the rest of this job as quickly as possible and get out of here.

It was just after eleven when they finished the final wall—one that was largely covered by cabinets. Katie jumped down from the countertop with a loud grunt. "At last. Looks good. Don't you think?"

He tried to concentrate on the question, nodding distractedly in response. His sense of unease was growing and he knew he had to say something to her about what had happened between them, to make sure nothing similar happened tonight.

He took her brush and washed both of them in the sink, while she pulled masking tape away from the trim. They finished the cleanup quickly, in silence.

"Katie," he said finally, as she was washing her hands. "We need to talk about what happened last night."

Not that, Katie thought. She should've known he'd turn it into a big deal. Some men couldn't just kiss, enjoy it and not *think* it to death. If there was one thing she couldn't stomach, it was "talking" about a relationship or for that matter, a simple kiss.

She tore off a paper towel and dried her hands. "What's there to talk about?"

"Mind if we sit out on the steps? I could use some fume-free air."

"Fine." She followed him out the front door and sat on the top step, leaving a good foot between them.

"What happened last night... It shouldn't have. It can't happen again."

That wasn't what she'd expected at all. "O-kay. Mind telling me why? It seemed like you were pretty into it at the time."

"Don't get me wrong, it was good. It was more than good." He glanced at her lips and she could tell by the look on his face that he meant it. "You're right. I was 'pretty into it.'"

She would've called him a liar if he'd tried to deny it. She was quite sure she'd never had a kiss that compared, and if she was feeling that way about it, chances were he was, too.

"So, then, what's the problem?" she asked.

He hesitated. "Remember I told you I'd lost someone I cared about?"

"Yeah?"

"You remind me of her. Far too much."

"I remind you of a dead woman?"

"No, you remind me of her when she was very much alive. She was reckless and impulsive. Loved high-risk activities. Took some dangerous chances and ended up losing her life because of it."

Katie tried to absorb what he was saying, but she didn't know what to make of it. She was terribly sorry his girlfriend had died. She couldn't imagine that kind of tragedy. She was still thrown off by her mom's death so many years ago, so she was in no position to think his reaction now was abnormal.

"Okay. So we can paint together but no kissing. Is that right?"

"I don't know." He buried his head in his hands. "I don't exactly know what I'm trying to say, other than getting involved with you… It scares the life out of me."

Several half thoughts swam through Katie's head. The one in the forefront was that he didn't want her around, so she wasn't going to stay here trying to convince him he was wrong. That was nuts. It was only a kiss, a few kisses—granted, they were kisses that had turned her inside out—but it wasn't worth arguing about.

"I'm leaving," she said, standing.

"Katie…"

She walked down the concrete steps toward her Jeep. "Good night, Noah."

Noah watched her leave. It bothered him more than he would have guessed. He'd had no doubt he was messed up, but this made him think he was in worse shape than he'd suspected. The plan had been to walk away from her and everything would work out okay. He'd distance himself from the state of cold panic that descended anytime he thought about the risks Katie put herself in and everything would return to normal.

He hadn't expected to feel any sadness watching her leave, knowing he'd hurt her on some level even if she was a strong woman who would never let a man break her down. Especially one she didn't even have a relationship with.

Yeah, he *was* messed up.

But it was done. He'd just scared Katie away from him for good. Which was what he'd set out to do. Wasn't it?

CHAPTER TWELVE

KATIE NEARLY FELL off her lawn chair when Noah strolled out of her dad's new house and onto the deck. Today. For her birthday dinner.

Judging by Noah's look when he was faced with Katie's entire family, he'd been left in the dark, too. Which made perfect sense, since he wanted nothing to do with her.

There were a couple of ways she could handle this. Be unfriendly and make him feel even more uncomfortable or…not.

Honestly, she wasn't mad at him. She was annoyed as all get-out, but she wasn't angry. She still had a couple things to say to him in regard to their conversation two nights ago, but now was not the time.

So she smiled and said hello. Her dad began introducing everyone—her sisters, their husbands and the kids—and Noah mentioned he'd met Lindsey, Zach and their boys out in the yard at his new house. He asked about Grandma Rundle, as well, who was having an "off" day and had stayed home with Annie, her caretaker.

"There are beverages in the cooler here and a seat over by the birthday girl," Mr. Salinger told Noah after everyone had been introduced.

Noah thanked him heartily, helped himself to a beer and then looked for the empty seat. He made his way to Katie's side and sat down as everyone went back to their own conversations.

"It's your birthday?" he asked her quietly.

"Don't tell me you forgot my present?" She leaned a little closer. "Or is my present just that you're talking to me?"

"Low blow. I had no idea it was your birthday or that you'd be here. Or that half of Lone Oak would be here. I ran into your dad at the hardware store last night and he invited me for dinner. I thought it was a retry from when he'd asked me a couple weeks ago."

"He's like that. Full of surprises, without intending to be. I didn't know you were coming, either."

"I can leave, if you're not comfortable having me here."

"Noah," she said, amused. "Do I look uptight?"

"You don't get uptight. I forgot." He tried to grin, as if he'd made a joke, but their fundamental differences were preoccupying both of them. "By the way, I wanted to thank you, again, for the painting help. The kitchen looks great."

"Not a problem. I like it, too. And it no longer looks like 'my' house."

Noah studied her. Made her feel as if no one else was around, his eyes understanding. "I don't imagine that fixed everything, though."

"Nope. I'm still basically as freaky as ever, where the house and my mom are concerned." Katie could legitimately see the humor in her problems, at least while she was surrounded by her family in the middle of the day. As Noah had commented recently, night was a different story.

He touched her arm, just for a couple of seconds. Katie bit her lip and said nothing. She could do without mixed signals. She stood up to break the contact and went inside to see if she could help Claudia serve dinner.

A couple of hours later, they'd devoured burgers and hot dogs, as well as so many side dishes that Noah thought Claudia could give his mom a run for her money in the party-hosting department.

He saw Katie slip inside again while everyone else was still eating. He'd finished his meal and thought now would be a good time to get out of Dodge. Katie likely didn't want him here, even though she'd gone out of her way to be friendly.

She was a class act. A lot of women would've caused a scene after their conversation the other night. He knew she didn't understand—they hadn't really talked enough for her to grasp exactly where he was coming from, and yet instead of being irrational and unpleasant today, she'd made him feel welcome.

Yeah, he really needed to do her the favor of disappearing.

Noah went inside, closing the door behind him to keep the air-conditioned air where it belonged. Katie was in the kitchen rinsing dishes.

"Hey," he said, and she jumped a little.

"Hey."

"I thought now would be a good time for me to take off."

She looked up at him. "You're leaving? Already?"

"It's been more than two hours since I crashed your party. I figured you couldn't wait to see me go."

"You're not bothering me. In fact, I think we have some things to talk about."

"Like what?"

"Us. Not kissing. Et cetera."

"Is there really anything else to say?"

"In case you hadn't noticed, I haven't

said much of anything. Yet. I was a little stunned the other night."

"Fair enough. When do you want to have this conversation?"

"Right now's good."

"You're kidding, right? You've got cake and presents coming."

Katie glanced at the kitchen table, covered with gift bags and colorfully wrapped boxes. She nodded. "I suppose you're right. Will you stay?"

"Are you sure you want me here?"

"Noah, I like you, strangely enough. I'm not going to send you away just because you went freaky on me."

"Freaky on you?"

She smiled. "Come on, admit it."

"You don't know what I've been through…"

"No. I don't. I'd like to, though."

"Now's not a good time."

"Yeah, I know. Presents. Cake. Why are we standing in here arguing again?"

"You called me a freak."

Katie laughed. "Will you stay?"

Noah was uneasy about returning to this conversation later, when they really got down to it, but he supposed he owed it to her. And the truth was that no matter how much he'd needed to cut off any kind of involvement at the pass the other night, he found he still cared about her.

"I'll stay. As long as you don't tell everyone else I'm a freak."

"Your secret's safe with me."

She closed the dishwasher and came to his side, wrapping her hand around his bicep as they moved to the door. Her touch affected him, no doubt about it. Apparently his nerve endings hadn't gotten the message about him having decided to be immune to Katie.

"I'm glad you're here. Even if you didn't mean to be."

Noah didn't say anything, wasn't sure what to say. Because what he was thinking right then—that in a different life he'd be tempted to sweep her up in his arms and kiss her senseless—didn't seem like quite the thing to throw at her.

"There they are," Zach said, so that everyone paid attention when they came back out on the deck.

"What have you two been doing?" Lindsey's tone suggested something similar to what had been on Noah's mind and he was glad he wasn't prone to blushing.

"Dishes, sister dearest. Get your mind out of the gutter."

"What's a gutter?" Logan asked, making the adults laugh.

Savannah started to explain about gutters on houses as Wendell stood up and declared it was time for cake.

Claudia disappeared for a couple minutes while dinner plates were being cleared. Then she emerged from the house carrying a tall, round layer cake with creamy frosting and two big candles—a two and a seven. Noah glanced at Katie, who reclined in a lounger next to him.

"Vanilla?" he asked in surprise.

Katie's eyes sparkled. "Red velvet cake with double-thick cream cheese frosting. My absolute favorite."

Savannah leaned over. "She gets it every year, too. Spoiled much?"

Katie shot Savannah a smug shrug. "I'm the baby. Spoiled with my favorite birthday cake is the one perk."

Savannah made a sarcastic choking sound as Claudia started singing "Happy Birthday." Everyone joined in for an off-key performance, followed by a second verse involving smelling like a monkey that was led by the under-ten brigade.

Katie closed her eyes and appeared to be making a wish. Noah would have loved to know what it was.

Towering slices of cake were served, with scoops of Neapolitan ice cream on the side. Noah chuckled to himself at the combination of flavors. How completely Katie it was.

Katie set aside her half-eaten dessert when Owen, Billy and Zach brought her the pile of presents that had been on the table inside. She made a big show of opening everything from her family, especially those gifts from the kids. For someone who led such a wild and independent life, she would've made a wonderful mother.

"Did you like the pretty necklace from me and Allie?" Logan asked.

Katie took her new *K* initial necklace from the table in front of her, then leaned forward and hugged him. "This necklace is one of my favorites. In fact, I like it so much I think I'll wear it right now. Could you help me put it on?"

She squatted down and turned around so her nephew could do the honors, balancing herself by putting her hands on Noah's knees. He tried not to think about the urge that overcame him—to take those hands in his and pull her onto his lap.

The heart pendant that she always wore drew Noah's attention and he wondered at its significance. Her eyes met his and he thought for a moment he could see the woman beneath the daredevil.

Then the little boy looped the new necklace around her neck and fiddled with the clasp for several seconds before he succeeded in fastening it. Katie stood and turned to thank Logan, letting him admire it, and Noah tried to get his thoughts under control.

Maybe sticking around to talk afterward wasn't such a good idea, after all.

CHAPTER THIRTEEN

NOAH WAS ALMOST at his SUV when Katie caught up with him.

"You're sneaking away?" she said, disbelieving.

"It looked like you might be there a while."

When they got to his vehicle, Katie jumped into the passenger side.

"Need a ride home or something?" Noah asked.

"No. I told you I have things to say to you. Are you *trying* to be frustrating or does that just happen on its own?"

Noah felt like a ten-year-old who'd ticked off his mom. "I sometimes masquerade as an enlightened species, pretending I'm a doctor, but when you get down to it I'm just one of those pesky males."

Katie stared at him, then smiled. "Sometimes you do surprise me, Dr. Fletcher."

He circled around to the driver's side and got in. "Where to, Queen Bee?"

"I don't know. I'm easy."

"Easy like a hurricane."

The tips of her lips curved upward. "You haven't kicked me out, though."

"Not yet."

"Wait a sec," Katie said. "If you don't mind taking me home later, let me grab my gifts and stick them in the back."

Noah pulled into the Salingers' driveway and helped her carry everything out.

"All set now?"

Katie nodded.

He backed out, unsure where to go. After a few blocks of aimless driving they were close to the park, so he pulled in there. They got out and walked toward one of the benches.

"I'm going to hit the restroom," Noah told her, maybe partially to stall the conversation. He left her sitting on a bench under a good-sized tree.

When he returned less than five minutes later, he found her hanging upside-down from the lowest branch of that tree, her cast swinging in the breeze just like the rest of her. His heart constricted, as he imagined what would happen if her legs, which she'd slung over the branch by her knees, slipped. She might land on her head or neck and be paralyzed for life. At the very least, she might break her fall with her broken arm.

"What on earth are you doing?" he asked, automatically shifting a hand to the back of his neck to massage it.

"Hanging out."

He held his tongue, realizing half of Katie's pleasure was in getting to him with stunts like this one.

She levered herself back up into a sitting position on the branch. He wouldn't have believed she could do it with just one strong arm, but she managed it. Made it look simple, in fact.

He turned his attention to the rest of

the deserted park as she crept toward the trunk to climb down. He couldn't watch.

When he heard her feet hit the ground, he spun toward her, his teeth clenched.

"Noah, it's a tree."

"You're already injured. And you're twenty-seven years old. Not seven."

"You're no fun."

She sat down on the bench and Noah sat beside her, refusing to take the bait.

"So," she said. "I'm calling your bluff."

His eyes widened and he glanced sideways at her. "What are you talking about?"

"The whole no-more-kissing thing. I don't think that's exactly what you want."

He groaned inwardly. "You can't accept that I'm not stumbling over my own two feet to kiss you?"

She laughed. "Wow. Got me there. I've just been sitting here stewing."

"I told you the other night how I feel—"

"No, you really didn't. But that's not my point, exactly. I don't want a serious conversation about where we're going. We aren't going anywhere. We have no future together. Right?"

"Right."

"Neither of us wants one. I'm leaving in a couple weeks."

He nodded. "So you think we should just pretend there's no problem?"

"Why does there have to be a problem? My point is that we've had some good times together and there seems to be a pretty strong attraction. Why are you over-thinking it and turning *me* into the woman who hurt you so badly?"

"I never said she hurt me."

"You didn't have to."

They were both silent for several minutes. Then Katie stood up and paced slowly in front of him, hands shoved into the front pocket of her sleeveless hooded shirt. "Will you tell me about her? What happened?"

"Why do you want to know?"

She sat back down on the bench, cross-legged, facing him. "You've listened to me carry on about my mom, Noah. I know I'm not very good at the friend thing, with men *or* women, but I've appreciated being able to talk to you about it. I just thought I'd offer you the same opportunity."

He leaned back on the bench, stretching his legs out in front of him. "I don't normally talk about Leah."

Katie nodded. "That's cool. If you don't want to, I understand. I don't usually babble about my mom to people I hardly know, either."

She watched him, studied his face, each of his features. She propped her elbow on her knee, as if she didn't plan to move anytime soon.

"Do you really want to hear about her?"

"Yes."

"It's not a happy story."

She said nothing. Just waited for him to tell her.

He sighed. "I met Leah on the mission in the Congo. She was a fellow physician. Full of life. Spontaneous and always looking for adventure. She loved to skydive and white-water raft."

"And *you* fell in love with her?"

"Fell hard."

Katie ran her fingers slowly along his arm, back and forth, wishing she knew how to show him how sorry she was.

"She loved adrenaline, loved the rush of emergencies, especially. She'd started out in an E.R. in L.A. Loved working on the mission because we were always on alert, waiting for the next crisis to arise, in the midst of treating dying people who hadn't had health care for years. She loved a good thrill and loved making a difference."

He swallowed and Katie sensed he was just getting started.

"She was a good doctor. Very good. Except for that impulsiveness… In the end, it was the desire to save one more life that got her into trouble."

"What happened?"

"Two kids turned up in the middle of the night. Somehow they got the message to her that their mother had been shot and needed care."

"So she went with them."

"She went against policy to do it. Didn't tell anyone, didn't ask for help. The situation in the area was volatile to begin with, and it had become even more so in the preceding week. We'd been forced to retreat two days earlier, move the medical camp south a few miles. Insurgents, rebels… Everyone was crazy. So many people had been shot, injured, blown to pieces. Leah walked right into that. Knowingly. To try to save the mother of those kids."

"How'd she break the rules?"

"She needed permission to go. And she knew that. It was too unsafe."

Katie closed her eyes and nodded, her stomach knotting up with tension.

"Anyway, she took off. It was still dark. Maybe, in some part of her brain, she thought the dark would keep her safe." He scoffed. "No. I take that back. I don't have a clue what she thought or *if* she thought. She just took off into the dark woods, to save a dying woman who was probably already beyond saving anyway."

"Then what happened?" Katie nearly

whispered, terrified of the answer but unable to keep from asking.

"When I woke up at dawn, I went looking for her. Looked everywhere. Couldn't find her. I grabbed the head physician and a couple others and started searching the area. We tried to stay low. We found a man who'd been hiding just off the road, who'd seen Leah. He pointed us in the right direction. Dr. Howard and I knew it was imperative to try to find her and get her out of wherever she was."

Katie barely breathed. Noah stared at the surface of the bench, and she wondered if he would continue.

"We located her by her screams. Knew it was her because she was begging for them to shoot her—in English. We made our way closer, then split up, hoping that would improve our chances of doing… something. *Anything* to get her out of there.

"The guys who had her—there were four of them—saw Howard first. One of them went toward him and chased him away with a knife, managing to nearly cut off two of his fingers. Kiss of death for a surgeon.

"A few minutes later, I was close enough to see them torturing her. I couldn't take any more and I screamed at him to stop. Stupid, right? But I wasn't thinking straight at the moment."

Katie couldn't imagine.

He closed his eyes and didn't speak for some time. "Then they shot her."

Katie felt sick to her stomach. She stood and paced, not knowing what to say or do.

There wasn't a sound except for a light, peaceful breeze, blowing the leaves in the trees. It was so calm here. No hint of the violence that was a daily part of life half a world away. *So deceiving.*

Shivering, she turned toward Noah and watched him. He didn't look at her, didn't even seem to know she was there. He stared sightlessly, the torment in his eyes proof that he was completely lost in the horrible memory.

She moved toward him, wishing there was some way to wipe all of this from his memory, to somehow make it all right for him. Time would help him, surely, but this was something he would never forget, never completely escape.

"Noah," she said, standing directly in front of him. "I'm so sorry. I don't know what to say."

"It's better to say nothing, believe me."

"Yeah, well... Maybe that's so." She held her hand out to him. "Let's walk."

He looked up at her with haunted eyes. Finally, he accepted her hand and got to his feet.

They'd walked nearly a mile along the jogging path when she began to talk. "That's the reason you don't think you're a hero, isn't it?"

His jaw clenched.

"When did that happen, in relation to finding the little girl?"

"I found her minutes after watching Leah die."

Katie nodded, thoughts flooding her head. After hearing the rest of Noah's story, she was more certain than ever that he was a hero, but telling him that right now wouldn't do any good.

"You've been through a nightmare," she said quietly.

"We both have."

Katie thought to herself that her nightmare had been a lot more mundane than his, no matter how much it had hurt. She absolutely couldn't fathom what he'd been through.

"Let's talk about something else," Noah said, still holding on to her hand.

"I don't know if this is better, but I'm curious... I understand that you think I'm similar to Leah, but why does that mean you can't kiss me?"

He eyed her sideways.

"I know I'm acting like my bulldog sister Lindsey, not letting this go, but the point has nothing to do with kissing. Or very little, at least. It actually goes beyond that."

They took several more steps before he asked, "Are you planning on enlightening me?"

She tried to figure out how to get into this without starting another argument. "It comes down to the way we live our lives."

"We're opposites," he said.

"One hundred percent."

"And you're going to tell me I need to lighten up and not focus on the past."

She tilted her head to the side, thinking. "No. Your past is pretty huge. I'm not in the position to tell anyone how to live. But...we're here right now because, well, we have some things in common. Right?

"I spend time with you because for some strange reason I like you. Even though your worrying makes me nuts and your need for control makes me want to pull my hair out. This was all prekissing, by the way."

"Prekissing. Gotcha."

"Why do you hang out with me?"

"Free labor? Milkshakes?"

She pretended to slug him in the gut.

"Okay, okay. Same thing you said. Even though you drive me nuts, I like you. Like your zest for life, your take on lots of things."

"I'm probably leaving in less than three weeks. So my question is, what is it going to hurt if we do continue to spend time together for a little while?"

He hesitated, opened his mouth to speak and then closed it again.

"Just say whatever you were going to say. We're being so uncomfortably honest I'm about to start hyperventilating," Katie said. "You might as well get it out."

Noah still took several seconds to speak. "When I'm with you, I spend half my time thinking about kissing you. Touching you."

Something deep inside Katie sprang to life at these words. She inhaled slowly and didn't look at him. "The same thoughts have occurred to me."

Part of her wanted the ground to open and swallow her. She'd never been so frank about such things in her life. Had never shared feelings very well. Didn't dare to think about why she could with Noah or why she was doing so now.

She heard Noah exhale shakily. "Well, then…"

Katie laughed nervously, then turned serious. "But you don't want to get any closer to me, because you're afraid something bad will happen to me—like it did to Leah."

He thought about it for a while, then nodded. "I guess that's part of it. The other part is that we have no hope of ever working out long-term."

"Are you looking for long-term?"

"Hardly. Not now. I've got too much to get through first. You?"

"What do you think?"

"I think you don't do serious or long-term, either."

"You think right. Ready to turn back?" She glanced up at the sky. "It'll be dark soon."

They stopped on the trail and turned around. Katie wasn't surprised when he didn't seek out her hand again. But she missed his touch.

"I'm throwing out a challenge," she said after several more minutes of silence. "I challenge you to see if you can let go and have some fun. With me. Until I leave town."

She waited for him to say something. Frankly, she expected him to cut down her suggestion right away. But he just walked. Thinking. Always thinking.

"We don't have a future together, and that's how we both want it. You won't have to spend a lifetime trying to convince me to quit jumping out of planes. I won't have to needle you to give it a try. We just have a couple weeks together to do what we want, just two adults who happen to enjoy driving each other crazy."

He tried to conceal a smile. "You make it sound so tempting."

She stepped in front of Noah, forcing him to stop or run her over. She brushed her index finger over his lips, then stood on her tiptoes, pulled his head to hers and kissed him.

Noah didn't fight it. And when she stepped away from him, the look he gave her made it extra difficult not to do it again. But she had a point to make.

"I don't want you slipping into something that makes you uncomfortable. But I do challenge you to have some fun. Conscious decision. And I realize it may be stepping out of your comfort zone. I'm just thinking that fishing might not completely do it for you." She grinned and resumed walking.

Noah was two steps behind her or so, watching her and pondering her "challenge." What he really wanted to do was turn her around and kiss her some more, but nothing had changed. He still couldn't simply give in to his desires, disregarding what his head was telling him.

He laughed inwardly. What man wouldn't give his left arm to spend time with this woman, no strings?

He refused to give in, though. Not right now. He needed to think about it more, because he'd found in the past he usually regretted the things he hadn't considered carefully. Such as kissing her the other night. It'd been a whim and, in the end, he'd wished he'd held on to his control.

They reached the end of the path quickly.

"Your brain's churning away, isn't it?" Katie asked with a knowing smugness.

"Why do you say that?"

"You're so quiet, I can practically hear the gears turning. I do know how you work."

"Guilty as charged. It's just…hard for me to let go."

"Oh, believe me. I know." Katie glanced over at the playground longingly. "I'm going to walk home. Think about it all you want. Ball's in your court."

She walked off without looking back. Surprisingly, she didn't head for the

merry-go-round, but left the park, heading toward her sister's home.

Noah couldn't help but notice that it was
extra quiet now that she was gone.

CHAPTER FOURTEEN

"I THINK YOU'LL be very happy here, Noah."
His mother inspected the stack of boxes
against the kitchen wall of his new home.

"Mom, no more unpacking. You've done
plenty already. Thank you."

Noah and his dad leaned against the
bare kitchen wall, as he didn't yet have
a table or kitchen chairs. The move had
been relatively simple, due to the fact that
most of Noah's belongings had already
been packed and in storage. Movers had
taken care of the heavy loading and unloading and his parents had spent most of
the afternoon here with him helping.

"The color looks wonderful," his mother
said. "Were the walls already that color or
did you have to paint?"

"I painted. The whole main floor, in
fact." He'd done the dining room and the

study by himself, one room per night, and by now he was sufficiently sick of the whole process.

"How did you get all that done without taking any time off work?"

"I had some help a couple of nights. Katie Salinger." She'd rarely left his thoughts since throwing down her challenge last night. Even in his sleep, she'd filled his mind.

His dad perked up. "Katie's in town?"

"She's been here for several weeks. Been in the office, as a matter of fact."

"Why didn't I know this? She was always one of my favorites." He removed his glasses and absentmindedly chewed on the end of an earpiece. "You must've taken care of her. Is she still accident-prone?"

Noah couldn't prevent a chuckle. "She came in because she'd popped twelve stitches."

His dad straightened. "You know, son, I ran into Harvey Eastman the other day at the diner. He said he'd been in to see *you*. For some reason, he couldn't get an appointment with me. And Katie— What's going on? Why are you stealing my patients?"

"Stealing your patients?"

"Why did Katie come to you instead of me, her doctor of twenty-some years?"

"You were probably busy. She didn't have an appointment. Walked in."

"Come to think of it, I haven't had more than about two walk-ins in as many weeks." He looked pointedly at Noah. "Son, you better tell me now what you're doing."

He could lie, but his dad would check it out Monday morning.

"I don't want you overdoing it, Dad. I asked Eve to give me the last-minute patients, in order to ease your load."

"I don't remember complaining about my load."

"No, you didn't. You take it and get it done. And that's part of the reason I had to talk to Eve. I knew if I mentioned it to you, you'd blow a gasket."

"Am I blowing a gasket now?"

"The steam is building."

"Noah, why did you think you could just go behind my back to do this?"

"You're sixty-three years old, Dad. Why do you think you need to work ten-hour days? You're running so hard to get it all done, that one of these days something's going to happen. You could have a heart attack."

"My heart is healthy."

"Noah..." his mom said from the sink, where she'd been tidying dishes that didn't need to be tidied. She turned off the water and moved closer to her son as she dried her hands on a dish towel she'd just dug out of a box. "What's going on with you? This sounds an awful lot like what you pulled with the housekeeping service."

"I'm trying to take care of you two, since you don't seem to notice you're getting older."

"Ivan, maybe we ought to check out the seniors' home in town. I hear they have bingo night right there in the social room.

We wouldn't ever have to take a step off the property."

"Mom, stop. Look at you two. When's the last time you both took some time off to relax?"

"This coming from our workaholic son?" she asked. "Noah, we've managed all by ourselves ever since you left home eighteen years ago. Yes, we're older now, but we're doing just fine."

Noah tapped his fingers on the Formica, wondering how much he could say without getting his mom bent out of shape. That was the last thing he wanted, but he also needed to explain himself.

"So, I'm a little hypersensitive. I worry about you two and I want to do whatever I can to make sure you stay healthy."

"This is because of what happened on your mission, isn't it?" his mom asked.

"This is because I care about you." That was partly true. Losing Leah had done a number on him. He found himself battling an overwhelming fear that something bad might happen to everyone else he cared about.

There'd been times when he'd woken up from his usual nightmares about the day Leah had died only to confront an irrational but overpowering worry that one of his parents was about to die.

Then there was Katie. He tried not to care about what happened to her, either, but he worried about her frequently. He'd still fret about her when she went back to St. Louis, back to her job and life. Back into frequent danger.

Now a black cloud of panic rose in his chest. He closed his eyes and tried to erase all the fear from his mind, taking deep, calming breaths.

"Son, I don't know everything that happened over there, but I realize you've been through something terrible. That'll mess with your mind without you even being aware of it."

He was more than starting to understand that. He recognized that his fear about his parents was not entirely justified, but that didn't prevent him from acting on it in the only ways he could think of. "I saw a psychiatrist about all this when I got back to the States. And I'm working through it. The fact remains, though, that the two of you shouldn't be spending your lives cleaning the house or sprinting between patients. You're getting close to retirement. So do me a favor and start thinking about how you'd like to spend your free time."

"I hope you're smart enough to know better than to try to push me out of the practice," his dad replied. "I can still fire you."

"I'm not pushing. I'm simply encouraging you to start preparing to make the change. In a few years. When you're ready."

"I'll think about it," his dad grumbled.

Noah straightened up, stretching out the kinks in his back. "Oh, and one more thing…"

Both parents looked at him, their faces so full of worry that he began to feel ill.

"Your new lawn-care company is showing up first thing Monday morning. No more mowing that huge lawn."

"That one I'll gladly take," his father said, to Noah's complete surprise. "I'm sick to death of all that grass."

Noah nodded, sick of it himself and he'd only been mowing it for a few weeks.

"Honey, I'm worried about you," Martha said, hanging her dish towel over a cupboard knob. "This fear you seem to have developed isn't normal."

She was too intuitive. "Mom, please don't start worrying about me. That'll just make me feel worse."

"You need to make some changes in your life, as well, and then maybe I'll try to slow down the worrying. But I'm still your mother, and I'll never stop worrying altogether."

"My life is fine…"

"Your life is all work," his father said. "You're worried about me having too many patients, but at least I go home at the end of the day and have a life with my wife. What do you do?"

"I'm going to start fishing." It sounded pointless even to Noah's own ears.

"You took the boat out once, two weeks ago. You don't even have a fishing pole."

"I'll get one."

"See that you do. You need to add some excitement to your life, otherwise you'll look older than your mother and me by the time you're forty."

He knew his parents were right, but knowing and doing something about it were two different things.

Katie had talked to him about conquering fears one of the first times they'd been together. It had struck him at that moment that fear had a heavy hand in his life. Still did, since he hadn't done a thing about it. Instead, he'd tried to push all of those disturbing thoughts from his mind.

It was true, though. His fears were controlling him. For a man who valued self-control as much as he did, that didn't sit well.

He'd shied away from Katie's offer, but

now he knew that taking her up on her plan could be the first step in getting his life back.

KATIE WAS FAR TOO excited to see Noah saunter into the crowd at Earl's.

She watched his progress from her booth in the corner, close to the stage. Half the town was here tonight, either because it was Saturday night or because of the band, and so she had to crane her neck to see him. Then she lost sight of him.

"Who have you got your eye on?" Lindsey asked suspiciously.

"No one." Katie returned her attention to her sisters. "I'll go get us a refill." She grabbed their empty pitcher and walked toward the bar, hoping to figure out where Noah had gone.

People were lined up four deep all the way around the bar, which gave Katie ample opportunity to look. But she didn't see Noah anywhere and began to wonder if her eyes had been playing tricks on her. What, after all, would the man be doing in a joint like this? She couldn't picture him whooping it up on Saturday night.

"You!" Eve was working her way toward Katie and gave her a hug. "Good to see you out and about. What's going on?"

"I'm hanging out with my sisters. What about you?"

"Stalking one of the bartenders." She nodded her head toward the good-looking one who was working the near end of the bar. "Totally not fun when the place is this busy."

Katie laughed and couldn't help looking around for Noah one more time.

"Are you the reason he's here?" Eve said, acting as if the light had just gone on in her head.

"Who's here?"

"Dr. Noah is here, and let me tell you, that's like finding a polar bear in the middle of the desert. He's gotta be here for a reason."

Katie tried to make her heart slow down and played dumb. "Why would I be the reason?"

"You know how offices are. Word gets around."

"There's really no word to get around. He bought my dad's house."

Eve's smirk said she knew better, so Katie changed the subject. They moved closer to the bar, discussing the band and the bartender that Eve was pursuing. It took a conscious effort on Katie's part not to look for Noah every two minutes, but she told herself that once she got back to her table she'd be able to spot him.

She finally got to the counter, ordered and waited for her pitcher. Eve's attention switched to the man behind the bar.

"You're a hard woman to track down."

The words, inches from her ear, sent a shiver down her spine and caused her pulse to skyrocket.

Katie turned her head to Noah, who was still just a whisper away from her. "What are you doing here?"

He took her injured hand, since the other one held a pitcher of beer, and pulled her gently out of the crowd.

"Trying to have fun," he said, directly into her ear again since that was the only way to be heard.

Katie looked at him, wondering whether that statement meant what she thought it did. His slow smile convinced her she was right.

"It's girls' night," she said full of regret. No matter how much she'd rather escape with him, this was her only chance to spend time with her sisters away from their families. "Salinger girls' night."

"So I heard."

She looked at him questioningly.

"Michael," he said.

"You went to Savannah's?"

He nodded. "I couldn't very well start my quest for fun if I didn't first track you down, could I?"

"You're scaring me," she said.

"Welcome to the club. Where are your sisters?"

She nodded her head toward their corner. Noah took her pitcher from her and forged ahead through the crowd, holding it high so it didn't spill. When they arrived at the table, he set it down.

"You're my hero," Savannah said, practically lunging for it.

"See?" Katie said to him. "You *are* a hero."

He squeezed her hand and said hello to her sisters.

"Wait. This is girls' night. And *you*—" Savannah squinted at him "—are not a girl."

"She's the brilliant one in the family," Lindsey said.

"I'm not staying," Noah said, smiling. "Which one of you drove?"

Lindsey raised her hand. "I have a feeling we'll be walking home, however."

"I have Katie's birthday presents from the other night in my SUV. Mind if we put them in your car?"

"Feel free." Lindsey dug her keys out of her purse and handed them to Katie.

It was a relief when they stepped outside and the door shut behind them, closing in the nonstop clamor. It hadn't bothered her before, but Katie was glad to be able to talk to Noah without having to shout.

He continued to hold her hand as they walked slowly toward the Tahoe.

"Savannah's having a good time, I see," he said.

Katie nodded. "I think she needs it. I'm worried about her."

"She's the reason you're still in town?"

Katie eyed him. "Absolutely."

He unlocked the back door and handed her several boxes and bags before grabbing the remaining ones himself. She led him to Lindsey's Civic, which was parked behind the bar.

Once they'd set her loot in the trunk, Katie slammed the lid shut and turned to Noah.

"So."

"So?"

"What's this about you being out to have a good time?"

He suddenly looked less sure of himself. Leaning against the trunk of Lindsey's car, he grasped Katie's hands and wove their fingers together. "I know you have to get back inside…"

"I've got time."

Instead of saying any more, Noah pulled her closer and kissed her. Katie's heart dropped into her stomach. He slid his hands around her back, leaving a trail of warmth wherever he touched her.

Katie wrapped her arms around him, wanting him nearer. She ran her fingers through the thick hair at his nape and over his broad shoulders.

Noah's hands circled her waist.

"You make me crazy," he whispered into her ear.

"I could say the same." Her breath was so shallow she could barely get the words out.

He pulled her into a tight hug, a groan in his throat. "You have to go back inside. I have to go home."

Katie smiled up at him. "I'm glad you came here. I figured you'd decided to blow off my challenge."

"I won't lie. I thought about it."

"What made you change your mind?"

"That's something we can discuss at a later time. Right now, you need to go baby-sit your big sister."

Katie chuckled. "She's in rare form." Her expression grew serious. "When you talked to Michael, did he seem upset?"

"He seemed…apathetic, really. Not at all upset she was gone."

"That's even worse." She chewed on her lower lip. "I have a very bad feeling about the two of them. He's hardly been home since I started staying there. Drags in after dinner. And Savannah's sleeping on the couch."

Noah frowned. "I hope they can work it out." He kissed her forehead. "Go have fun."

"Thanks for interrupting."

"My pleasure." He walked her to the door and kissed her again quickly. Katie was already contemplating the next time she could see him.

CHAPTER FIFTEEN

KATIE HERDED LOGAN and Allie through the back door after a trip to the city pool the following day. Normally Savannah took them swimming, but she was paying for her night out in more ways than one. Not only did she admit to a raging headache, but Katie doubted she'd gotten much sleep. She'd heard Savannah arguing with Michael for a good half hour after they'd gotten home.

Not knowing what else to do, Katie had offered to take the kids to lunch and then swimming. They'd been gone for several hours and she hoped that Savannah had grabbed a nap.

But clearly, Savannah hadn't. And clearly she didn't feel better.

Katie was the first through the doorway connecting the kitchen to the living room. Her sister was slouched on the most uncomfortable chair in the room, her eyes red and full of tears.

Katie's stomach dropped. "What's wrong?" she asked, then quickly held up her index finger and turned to Logan and Allie. "Kids, get your swimsuits off and then head out to the backyard. You can play outside until dinner."

They were too revved up to pay attention to their mother and bounced through the hallway to their rooms. But Katie had a premonition of disaster.

"Savannah, what's going on?"

"He left."

Katie kneeled on the floor in front of her sister. "He left," she repeated, confused. "Michael? Where'd he go?"

Savannah shrugged. "I don't know. He left me."

Understanding dawned. "*Left you* left you? Oh, Van. What happened?"

For the first time in her life, she watched Savannah break into quiet sobs. Katie grasped her hand and rubbed her forearm, her heart aching for her sister.

"Don't…wanna…talk," Savannah said between gasps.

Katie soothed her for a long time. When the kids emerged from their rooms, she made sure they went straight outside, blocking Savannah from their sight as best she could. One thing at a time. If Michael had left, the kids would need to know. But not this second.

"Are you sure he's not coming back?" she asked once the door had slammed. "Maybe he was just mad."

"He wasn't mad. He was calm. So horribly calm about walking out the door… with all his clothes in suitcases." Savannah sniffled loudly, then blew her nose. She sat up straighter. "No more crying."

"Cry all you want to. Get it out."

"I've been crying for the past two hours. Lot of good it's done." Her voice was stronger, as if she was now determined to stay in control. That was more the Savannah Katie knew.

"Did you guys have a fight or what?"

Savannah shook her head, dazed. "I messed it up."

"Messed what up?"

"My entire freaking marriage."

"No. You didn't, Savannah. It takes two."

Savannah shook her head more emphatically. "Nope. This was all my doing. And now he doesn't love me anymore."

"I don't believe that." Katie's response was automatic, but when she thought of the interaction between her sister and Michael lately, she wasn't so sure she was right. "Why don't you tell me what happened."

Savannah stood, making a frustrated, angry grunt. She paced across the room and back. "A couple months ago, Michael told me he didn't love me anymore. It came out of nowhere."

"I don't get it. Is he involved with someone else?"

"Not that I know of." She pulled her long hair up with both hands, sighed deeply and then let it fall again. "He said he can't stand the way I control every bit of our lives. I'm a control freak."

"You've been a control freak since you were born. He knew that going into your marriage."

"Yeah, well, apparently at some point he decided he couldn't live with it."

"Why now?"

Savannah tried to laugh, but the sound came out bleak and defeated. "He's grown to resent me so much that he couldn't stand to stick around any longer. Not even for the kids."

"Oh, Van." Katie wanted to hug her sister, but Savannah's stance told her she wouldn't be receptive to any kind of contact right now.

"When he first told me all this, I convinced him to stay. We tried counseling a couple of times. But it didn't work out. The counselor basically said that we had too much to overcome and Michael didn't have the will to try. He really hates me."

"Why didn't he bring this up five years ago, so you wouldn't end up like this?"

"Oh, he may have tried. He's told me I'm too controlling before."

"And?"

"And nothing. I just didn't realize it was really a matter of, 'You're a control freak and you need to change or I'll come to hate you.' I know, I'm an idiot."

"You are not. He should've tried harder to make you understand."

"I should've backed off." Savannah sprawled on the couch. "I thought I was doing it right. He didn't want me to work until the kids were older. So I made this house my job. Our lives."

"You've been super wife," Katie admitted. "Look at this place. You do everything, coordinate everything, schedule, cook, clean, plan. Savannah, all he had to do was come home from work and be a part of the family. Was that so horrible?"

Savannah nodded and leaned forward, running her hands through her hair again. Her head was bowed, her face hidden.

Katie wondered if she was crying again. Then Savannah pushed back her hair and stood in one quick motion. She strode to the doorway. "I'm so stupid!" As she said the words, she punched the doorjamb with the side of a fist. Hard enough to make Katie flinch and wonder if she'd damaged the wood.

"You're not stupid, Savannah. If you say that again, I'm going to kick you."

Savannah slowly turned around to face her, breaking into a semihysterical laugh. "No, you're not. Because I'm a control freak and you will not touch me!"

Katie wasn't so good at handling hysteria. "Why don't we call Lindsey and have her come over?"

"Why? So she can ask me twenty questions? I'm pretty much talked out."

"Have you spoken to a lawyer at all?"

"Yeah. That was my secret errand in Topeka."

"You could've just told me, you know."

Savannah's head drooped and she leaned against the door frame. She held up her hand and was clearly in pain. It was as if she'd just now noticed how much it hurt.

"Your wrist's already swelling. That's not good," Katie said.

Savannah shrugged.

"Go sit down or lie down. Put some ice on it. I'm going to make sure the kids are okay, then we'll figure out what to do next."

Katie nearly fell over in shock when Savannah actually did as she'd been told. She hurried to the back door and looked outside. Allie was in the sandbox making a sand castle, and Logan was swinging upside-down on the old metal play set, hollering at his sister, who was ignoring him. All was right in their world. At least for now.

Not so in Katie's, however. She needed to be the strong one for Savannah. But— the thought of losing Michael from their family, of Savannah losing her husband, of Logan and Allie losing their father...

She leaned against the kitchen wall for support. She hated thinking about all the changes there were likely to be in everyone's future. Closing her eyes, she forced that line of thought away for now. This wasn't a good time to lose it.

Straightening, Katie picked up the phone and carried it around the corner, onto the top landing of the basement stairs. She dialed Lindsey and, speaking in a rushed whisper, asked her to come over, telling her only that Michael had walked out.

When she returned to the living room, Savannah was sitting on the edge of the couch, her injured wrist resting in her lap and her attention obviously elsewhere.

"Savannah, we have to have that checked out. Your wrist is already twice its normal size."

Savannah glanced down at it and shrugged. "What am I going to say to the kids?"

Good question. "We'll figure that out. Lindsey's on her way over, and she's good at that kind of thing. But first we need to take you to the doctor."

"You're just looking for an excuse to see Noah. He'll love that bikini top."

Katie laughed in disbelief while realizing she did need to put on some clothes. "I don't need an excuse. I do, however, have a little experience with injured wrists and I'm thinking that yours could be broken. We'll take you in."

"It's Sunday. They're not open."

"I'll call Noah."

"I need to talk to the kids."

"We'll tell them when we get back. Go wash your face and get a drink."

"Oh, that'll solve all my problems." But Savannah got up and walked tiredly to her bedroom.

"I'm going to change clothes. We'll leave when Lindsey gets here."

Katie went downstairs and put on a halter and some shorts, ran a brush through her hair and then headed back upstairs. She heard Lindsey come in the back door.

"Hey," she said in a hushed voice, trying to catch Lindsey before she got to Savannah. "Thank goodness you're here."

"What in the world is going on?" Lindsey asked.

Katie filled her in on the few details she had to work with. "I'm taking her in to have her wrist checked out. Maybe wait till we get back to question her? She's… not exactly in a talkative mood."

"I can just imagine. Do the kids know anything yet?"

Katie shook her head no. "I don't have the first clue about what to say."

"We'll take care of that later. Go get her wrist examined."

The clinic was deserted and Katie was pretty sure that coming in on a Sunday for a minor emergency wasn't the norm. But when she'd called Noah, he told her to meet him there in fifteen minutes.

"Hello, ladies," he said, and the private look he gave Katie melted her insides. "What can I do for you?" He led them back to one of the exam rooms.

Katie pointed to Savannah's wrist. "She punched the doorjamb. Hard."

"I'm going to throw up." Savannah bolted out of the room.

"Her husband left her today," Katie told Noah, when Savannah was out of earshot.

"Your suspicions were right, then."

"Not even close. I had no idea it was *this* bad."

"Sounds like she's taking it hard."

"That'd be an understatement. Savannah has a huge amount of pride. I expect that's hurting her as much as suddenly being alone, a single parent. A divorcée-to-be. I don't think those things have even hit her yet."

"How are you holding up?" His voice was so gentle and caring, she shivered.

"I'm okay. Well, a little messed up, but I'll be okay."

"Messed up?"

Katie stood and stuck her head out the door to see if she could spot Savannah. "They've been together forever. Michael's always been like an older brother to me. Especially when I was still living at home." She stuck her hands in the back pockets of her shorts. "If *they* can't make it work…" She shook her head, not wanting to voice the thought that maybe no one could.

Noah could see that this was weighing on Katie more than she admitted. He couldn't relate to what she was going through, being an only child and having had no experience with divorce, but just from spending time with her family on her birthday, he knew Savannah's failed marriage would affect every single one of the Salingers.

His main concern was Katie, though. And Savannah's wrist, of course. But Noah hated to see Katie so sad and so involved in her sister's problems.

He was just about to move closer and give her a hug, when Savannah burst back into the room.

"Let's get this over with. I need to get out of here," she said, climbing up on the table and holding out her arm.

KATIE WAS DRAINED. She, Lindsey and Savannah had just tried to explain to Logan and Allie what was happening, and it had been even more difficult than they'd expected it to be. Logan was still wailing and Allie had lapsed into an eerie silence. Katie held the little boy and let him sob against her shoulder, her heart aching. The agony of losing a parent had come rushing back to her. It didn't seem to matter much that Michael wasn't dead and that he could still have contact with the kids. Logan and Allie's world would never be quite the same again.

Savannah looked as if she were about to collapse. Noah had given her some pain pills and a temporary wrap, and he'd suggested she keep ice on her wrist to reduce the swelling. The X-ray hadn't shown any break, however, so she was lucky in that regard.

"Why don't you go lie down?" Katie said to her. "Those pills will make you drowsy and you look about ready to fall over."

Savannah nodded, her eyes glazed. She came over and took Logan from Katie's arms and carried him into the living room, away from the others. Katie heard her talking quietly to her son and eventually he stopped crying enough to listen.

Savannah was a good mother, more so than Katie had ever expected her to be. Growing up, she'd been the least nurturing, the least caring, of the three sisters. She still sometimes came across that way to outsiders, but her children were the be-all and end-all of her existence and she would do anything for them. Katie just hoped they would come through this okay. Maybe coddling her kids would help Savannah to cope, as well.

Someone knocked on the front door and Katie jumped. "I'll get it," she called, not wanting anything to disturb Logan's time with Savannah.

Noah stood on the front porch. "Hello," he said.

"Hey." Katie came all the way outside, closing the door gently behind her.

"How's the war scene?"

"Kind of ugly. We told the kids not too long ago."

"You look worn out. I'm guessing you've had a long day."

She smiled slightly at the understatement. "You could say that."

"Have you eaten yet?"

Katie shook her head.

"Is Lindsey still here?"

"Yep, she's with Allie right now, who's giving us all the silent treatment."

Noah frowned. "She's at an age where it'll be especially tough."

"What age isn't tough to have your parents break up?"

"That's a good point." He shoved his hands into the pockets of his jeans. "Why don't you come with me? Get away from things for a while. We'll grab some dinner."

His offer was appealing, *really* appealing. Sitting around here for the whole evening might have her climbing the walls. But she couldn't just walk out while her family dealt with a major problem. This was why she'd remained in Lone Oak. "I need to stay."

As she spoke, the door opened behind her and she turned to see Lindsey and Allie. "We're going to cook dinner," Lindsey said. "I was going to ask if you two would join us, but it sounds like Noah just invited you out."

"I'm staying," Katie said.

"Go ahead and do it. The way I figure, you're going to be on night duty since you're sleeping here. I'll make dinner and then get the kids into bed and you can take over later on. Someone will always be here if Savannah needs something."

"I don't need anything," Savannah called from inside the house.

"Of course not," Katie said dryly, as she exchanged a look with Lindsey. "You really don't mind if I take a break?"

Lindsey shook her head. "Go. Enjoy it."

CHAPTER SIXTEEN

"WHERE ARE WE GOING?" Katie asked a few minutes later. Noah was driving in the opposite direction from his new home.

"I need to pick up my parents' lawn mower first. They're letting me borrow it until I can buy one. It shouldn't take long to retrieve it."

They rode in silence the rest of the short trip. When Katie got out of the truck in the Fletchers' driveway, Noah came around and took her hand in his, which was a little strange. If his parents saw this, it wouldn't just be a short, friendly visit. It'd be *You're dating our son, let's talk.* Katie wasn't prepared for that, even though she knew his father well from all those years of being one of his best patients. She wasn't dressed for it, either, since she was still wearing her halter, shorts and flip-flops.

But she shouldn't have worried. When they walked into the kitchen, she immediately felt at home. Noah introduced her and Dr. Ivan Fletcher jumped to his feet, smiling broadly.

"My goodness, you're all grown up. And still into trouble, I see." He motioned toward her wrist.

"But healing, thanks to the excellent medical care I've found in Lone Oak," she said.

Dr. Fletcher came over and hugged her. "What are you doing with this guy? I thought you were a hotshot reporter, out gallivanting across the country."

"They don't think much of casts and stitches when we're covering extreme sports," Katie said. "I work for *Rush* magazine, so pretty much everything's extreme."

"I know where you work. You've written some dandy articles, my dear."

"You've read them?"

"Of course, I have. We subscribe to the magazine at the clinic."

"You kids have dinner plans?" Mrs. Fletcher asked.

"We kids don't," Noah said dryly. "I came to get the lawn mower and then we'll grab something."

"We'd love it if you'd join us," Mrs. Fletcher said. "I was just about to start a stir-fry. I've got plenty of food."

Noah glanced at Katie, his eyebrows raised in question.

"Sounds good to me," she said.

"What can we do?" Noah asked.

"Go load the lawn mower. By the time you get finished and washed up, dinner will be just about ready."

Half an hour later, Noah sat with Katie and his parents at the table, all of them chatting as if Katie had been joining the other three for dinner for a decade. It was all fine with Noah, except for the fact that his mother was taking pleasure in regaling Katie with stories from his childhood, as she probably would with a serious girlfriend or fiancée. He had made a point of explaining that Katie was only in town for a couple more weeks, but his mother was very persistent.

And she wasn't being nearly as exasperating as his father was. They'd finished dinner and now his dad had dragged him out to the garage to show him which trimmer he could borrow. The man had four of the things, but then he'd always been overzealous about power tools—an interest Noah had never shared. He'd be grateful to have this one machine to make yard work faster and easier, though. He certainly didn't have a lot of spare time—or desire—to do lawn maintenance.

"What is Katie Salinger doing with you?" the senior Dr. Fletcher asked with an annoying gleam in his eye.

"Doing? Having dinner, Dad. That's all."

"She's special, son. I hope you treat her that way."

"We're not together. Not the way you think."

"I may be close to retirement age, but

I'm not dumb. I can see the interest. In both of you."

"I like her. She's fun to spend time with."

"You'll have to be careful with her. You can't control her, the way you like to control everything. She was always an independent one."

Noah stopped short as he was loading the trimmer. He set the thing down and turned to his father. "What are you carrying on about?"

"You've got control problems. I just don't see an independent spirit like Katie Salinger taking that from a man."

Noah chuckled, shaking his head. "Katie's leaving town in two weeks. She and I are *not* involved the way you seem to think we are." Not that his dad needed to know about, anyway.

Mr. Fletcher leaned against the side of the garage, crossed his legs at the ankle and chuckled. "Just be careful with her. I like her."

Noah shot him one more aggravated

look, then finished loading the trimmer and headed to the house.

He found the two women cleaning the kitchen together.

"Noah, you have to show me the rope swing by the river," Katie said. "Your mom's been telling me all about it and it sounds like a blast."

"Not for people with casts, it isn't."

"I just want to see it. Maybe when you take this thing off we can come back and try it out."

"You two take a walk, relax. Your dad and I have plans to watch a movie upstairs and retire early. Enjoy the evening."

"Let's go, then."

Katie grabbed her purse and slung the long strap over her head and one shoulder, then smiled and preceded Noah out the door.

"Did you get all your manly toys sorted out?" Katie asked, as they made their way through the huge backyard toward the grove of trees that hid the swing and the old boathouse on the bank of the river.

"The mower and trimmer are ready to go, although I've never considered power tools 'toys.' That's my dad's domain." He grimaced. "He just gave me some prime unsolicited advice."

"Oh, no. Dare I ask what?"

"He told me to be careful with you. Not to try to control you."

"Excellent advice." She wrinkled her forehead. "Does he think we're…together?"

"I assured him we're not, at least not the way he's thinking. You know, long-term."

She sidled closer and he twined their hands together, trying to ignore the way his heart rate sped at her touch.

They walked the rest of the way to the riverbank without talking, Noah utterly absorbed in the moment. And maybe she was, too. He could only hope.

When they got to the bank, he dropped her hand—reluctantly—and headed to the fat trunk of the oak tree where the swing had been tied up for years. He couldn't remember the last time he'd come out here to soar over the water.

The rope was brittle and a challenge to untie, but he finally released the swing from its hold and showed it to Katie. It had a simple plastic circular base with a hole in the middle of it and the rope knotted on the bottom.

"I love it! I want to give it a try."

"Too bad you hang out with your doctor."

A pouty look crossed her face. "Demonstrate. Please?"

How could he resist a plea from her? Besides, he was feeling just good enough to think a swing over the water sounded like the thing to do. Before she could ask him again, he took hold of the rope with both hands and hopped on, flying out far over the lazy river.

Katie whooped and hollered, moving onto the short dock to watch. He loved it when she was this happy. A childlike joy came over her face and he'd almost have thought she was the one floating back and forth through the air.

"One more week till this cast comes off. Then it's my turn," she said a few minutes later, after he'd expertly jumped from the swing onto solid ground beneath the tree.

Noah laughed. "You've jumped out of airplanes and off of mountains, and you still think a little river swing sounds exciting?"

"Sounds like the most exciting thing in Lone Oak, actually." She made her way off the dock and back onto the patchy grass where he stood. "So do you normally jump into the water instead of swinging back to the bank?"

"No. I'm not sure I've ever tried that."

"What? You're kidding me. Clearly you've led a sheltered life." She moved closer and ran her good hand up his chest, then curled both arms around his neck.

The swing dropped from Noah's hand and he didn't even glance at it as it swept back out over the water. There'd be no way to retrieve it without getting wet, but right now he didn't care. He barely registered it at all as he leaned nearer to Katie's lips, mesmerized by her spell, her scent, the mischievous gleam in her eyes.

"You let go of the swing," she said in a breathy whisper.

"What swing?" He touched her waist and slid his hands around her back as his lips met hers.

CHAPTER SEVENTEEN

WHEN KATIE SIGHED and leaned into him, Noah let a groan escape. Something about kissing her felt like he'd been doing it forever, yet at the same time, it was completely new and exciting.

Maybe he just needed to get out more. Go on dates.

The thought was fleeting and immediately dismissed, because the only thing he really wanted was to hold Katie in his arms for the next, oh, three weeks or so.

This woman had him under a spell and all he could think about was being close to her. He'd never felt anything this overpowering from just a kiss.

It had never been like this before. The intensity, the sweetness, the laughter. He and Leah hadn't had...this, exactly. He shouldn't compare, but Katie had managed to dim the painful memories so much after only a couple of weeks.

Katie pressed her cheek to Noah's chest, eyes closed, taking in the scent of him. An odd thought flitted through her hazy mind. Stability. Safety. Noah was both.

She knew she should run.

But somehow she couldn't drag herself away from the contentment and security that enveloped her, right now.

She moved to wrap her arms more securely around his neck and knocked him in the chin with her cast.

"No fair using that thing as a weapon," he said.

"Sorry." She kissed his chin to make it better, then held up her arm. "Think it will be good as new when you take this thing off?"

"Your arm should be fine. We'll check you out thoroughly before giving you the go-ahead."

"But what are the chances of it not being strong enough?"

"Odds are low that you'll have any problems."

"I talked to my boss today. Found out one of my first assignments when I get cleared. A rock climb in Colorado, the weekend of the twenty-fifth."

Noah would not allow himself to think about Katie rock climbing. "There's a seminar on pediatric food allergies in Denver—I'm almost sure it's the same week."

"You going?"

"I don't think so. Too much to do here."

"Too bad. You could watch me climb."

That was enough to set off the pressure in his head, the tension in his neck that had become so familiar to Noah. Watching Katie perform her daredevil antics was something he'd never be able to do. He'd grown to care far too much for her. He'd likely end up having an all-out anxiety attack just seeing her prep for the event.

"I don't think so."

"What are you so afraid of? Safety is my top priority when I'm on the job. I may get paid beans, but the magazine spares no expense when it comes to taking precautions."

Noah pulled away slightly, looking down into Katie's face. "We're having fun until you leave. Nothing else. Right?"

She studied him, then nodded. "Right. No talk about the future."

"No talk about you risking your life."

"I'm going to be fine."

"That's the deal. I'm doing my best not to think too much—just to live in the moment."

"Okay," she said, seeming to relent. "No talk about the other half of my life. We'll just pretend that Katie's a dull girl."

"That's not what I mean."

"I know what you mean. It's cool. Present only. No mention of the future." She nodded again, nearly convincing him she meant it when she said it was "cool." But there was a hint of irritation in her tone and he didn't know what to do about it.

"We need to get you back to your sister's."

"Yeah," she agreed. "Back to reality."

They made their way to his Tahoe, holding hands, kidding and tackling only light, safe topics. When he dropped her off at Savannah's, she leaned across the seat and kissed him sweetly. Then she was gone.

CHAPTER EIGHTEEN

WHEN KATIE WALKED into Savannah's kitchen, both her sisters stared at her wordlessly.

"What?" she asked.

"Have a nice dinner?" Lindsey asked.

"Yeah. Great dessert, too."

Lindsey chuckled. "We were about to call out a search party for you."

"I'm here now. You can go."

"I don't need a babysitter, guys. I'm fine," Savannah said. "Well, all but my wrist."

"How's it feeling?" Katie pulled out the chair next to Savannah and glanced at the protective wrap around it.

"The pills are making me loopy, but they're not actually killing the pain. I want a refund."

"They'll help you sleep, though."

"I have to go," Lindsey said. "Owen and Billy wait up for me even when they're not supposed to. It's a little late for seven-year-olds to be awake." Lindsey grabbed her purse from the counter. She put her arms around Savannah.

"Linds, I'm okay." Savannah scowled. "The bright side is, I get my own bed back tonight." Her scowl faltered and Katie wondered for a moment if her hard-as-nails sister was going to start crying again.

"Night," Katie said, hoping to hurry Lindsey out of there. Sometimes their doting older sister actually made things worse by being so…doting.

"I'll call in the morning." Lindsey looked back from the doorway.

"Not too early," Katie and Savannah said at the same time, then smiled at each other.

"How are the kids?" Katie went to the fridge to find a drink.

"Shell-shocked." A word that did a pretty good job of describing Savannah as well, from the look of her. "Bedtime was pretty awful."

Katie frowned, her heart tying itself in a knot. She remembered how, after their mom had died, she'd always felt most alone at night, as she was drifting off to sleep. "Sorry I wasn't here for that."

"Yeah, um—" Savannah leaned forward, elbows on the table "—where were you, exactly?"

Katie pictured Noah swinging out over the river and smiled. "If I told you, you wouldn't believe me."

Savannah studied her with interest and a halfhearted smile. "Well, at least one of us had a good day."

"Hard to call it good, after what happened here."

"Are you guys getting serious?"

"No," Katie answered without hesitation. "Definitely not. I go back to St. Louis in two more weeks."

"That's a lot of protesting."

"I don't do serious, remember? Frankly—" Katie leaned back and stretched her legs out on one of the empty chairs "—what you're going through now is exactly why."

Savannah shut her eyes briefly, then ran her thumb and forefinger from the outer corners of her lids to the bridge of her nose. After the past couple of days, the past couple of weeks even, Katie was starting to recognize something she hadn't understood before. Ever. Savannah had feelings that ran deep, just like everyone else, even though she spent the majority of her life hiding them. Acting invincible. And for the first time, Katie understood she *wasn't* invincible. It was all just that—an act.

"I shouldn't have said that," Katie said. "I'm sorry."

Maybe it was because Katie was the youngest sister. She'd grown up buying into the facade Savannah presented, that she was never hurt or sad or lonely. When their mom died, Lindsey had turned into a mother hen. Katie had been determined to be self-sufficient. But Savannah… She'd acted as if it didn't bother her. She'd turned into the rebellious one, the only one who dared to fight with their dad even when he was consumed with grief.

Katie realized now, she'd taken Savannah's anger as invincibility. All these years.

"I need to go to bed," Savannah said, pulling herself to her feet.

Katie stood, too, wrapping Savannah in a tight hug. "You're going to get through this just fine. You're a strong person, Van."

When she loosened her hold on her sister and looked into her eyes, she saw doubt, fear.

"I don't feel strong at all." She swiped at a tear. "I hate this. I feel so… I'm just really tired of crying."

Katie nodded. "If you can't sleep and want to talk…or *not* talk, come downstairs and get me."

Savannah nodded and they headed off in their separate directions.

"Katie."

Katie paused on the landing at the top

of the stairs and looked across the kitchen at Savannah.

"I'm glad you're here. I don't need a babysitter, but thanks for staying."

Katie smiled sadly and headed downstairs, able to agree with her sister on one thing. She was glad she was here, too. Glad she could help today, even if all she'd been able to do was drive Savannah to the doctor and hold her hand when she needed it.

She was so used to putting distance between herself, her family and her former life here in Lone Oak that the realization threw her for a loop.

NOAH WALKED OVER to where Katie sprawled on the couch looking prettier than ever in a little tank top and shorts, her cheeks flushed and her lips swollen from his kisses.

The image would remain with him long after she left town.

The thought of her leaving roused a worry he'd been shutting down for the past few days, unable to think about anything post-Katie just yet. He'd taken living in the moment to a new high—out of necessity.

He was falling for her. Why couldn't he just have fun, keep anything too deep out of the picture? He was frustrated with himself, as well as with the impossibility of a future with this woman.

"Hey," she said, looking up at him. She had a magazine opened in front of her, *National Geographic,* if he wasn't mistaken. "These guys amaze me."

"What guys?" He sat on the edge of the couch, close to her.

"These people who climbed Everest. Did you read this?" She tapped the magazine pages. "They had just about everything that could go wrong, go wrong, but they still made it. To the top. Totally inspiring."

"Sounds like a big game of chicken."

"And they won! Can you imagine what it must feel like to finally make it to the top, especially after all the trials?" She sat up, animated.

"I can't imagine why anyone would want to try."

"Someday I'm going to. It's something I've always wanted to do, ever since ninth grade, when I had to write a report about Edmund Hillary."

He narrowed his eyes, wondering if she was just goading him. "Why would you want to do that, Katie? Do you know how many people die trying?"

"One in eight. The point here is to not to be that one."

The flippancy in her tone set his nerves on edge, made him want to shake some sense into her.

"The body isn't meant to undergo something like that. Anyone who tries it deserves whatever he gets."

"The spirit of adventure lives in Noah Fletcher," she said dramatically.

"What do you think their families went through while they were climbing a mountain that was never meant to be climbed?"

"I'm sure they were worried, just like

they would be if they took a plane somewhere or caught the flu."

"Talk about a dumb, pointless endeavor that proves nothing but luck. You're
smarter than that, Katie. Tell me you're not
serious about this."

Katie glared at him. "Oh, I'm serious
about it. Like I said, it's one of my dreams.
And I can promise you no one will stand
in the way of my doing it." She got up and
started gathering her things.

As irritated as Noah was, he didn't want
her to leave. Their time together was lim-
ited enough. "Don't tell me you're going
home over this little dispute."

"Little dispute? Do you have a dream,
Noah? Anything you aspire to accomplish
one day? Why don't you tell me about it
so I can stomp all over it?"

She stormed away, vanishing through
the front door. Noah instantly regretted
letting his fear get the better of him. Why
bother fighting with her about something
she might or might not do in the future?
It wouldn't be his business or his prob-

lem because he'd be long out of her life by then.

But he'd let a knee-jerk reaction take over and push her away. Dumb move.

KATIE MARCHED UP Savannah's driveway toward the back of the house. She stopped, her hand on the doorknob, reconsidering. She was in no mood to act as if nothing was wrong, so she quietly let go of the screen door and took a seat at the patio table.

So much for a relaxing evening with Noah. She shuddered. What was with the relaxing evening stuff, anyway? That so wasn't her. She and Noah had slipped into some kind of domestic make-believe world and Katie hadn't even thought about it until now.

She'd spent the past few evenings at his house, although she always came back to Savannah's place for the night. She'd let herself get far too comfortable at Noah's place, something she never did. In fact, she usually made sure that the time spent with a man was on her terms, in her domain. But right now, she didn't really have a domain other than her apartment in St. Louis. And Noah's, well... It felt like hers. His territory was her former territory and somehow she'd let herself believe that getting comfortable there wasn't a problem.

Good thing he'd prompted a reality check.

Katie heard the back door opening behind her and didn't need to look to know who it was.

"I thought I heard someone out here," Savannah said as she sat down next to Katie.

"I'm back. Sorry for being gone so much. Lapse in judgment."

"What's going on? What are you doing out here?"

"Beating myself up."

"Oh, can I join?"

"Depends. Do you want to beat me up or yourself?"

Savannah shrugged. "I've beat myself up plenty lately. Might be interesting to branch out a bit. So what are we beating you up for?"

Katie snorted indelicately. "Being dumb."

"Can you be a little more specific?"

"Noah and I had an argument."

"Not good."

"I told him that I want to climb Mt. Everest someday. He called it a stupid endeavor."

Savannah just watched Katie.

"You don't tell someone their dream is stupid."

"Interesting," Savannah said, settling back into her patio chair.

"What's interesting?"

"Why do you care what Noah thinks?"

"Why wouldn't I?"

"You care about him more than you want to. You're not just mad he put down something important to you. You're mad you care so much."

"What he and I have is a temporary thing, just something to pass the time. We're supposed to be having *fun*."

Except obviously they weren't. Not tonight. That realization stung, because what if Savannah was right? Katie hadn't set out to care deeply. That wasn't the way she operated.

"If I told you that climbing a mountain was a dumb idea, you'd laugh and walk away," Savannah said.

Katie shook her head, denying it. "I'd be mad at you, too."

"I don't think so. Sure, you'd tell me off, but you wouldn't stomp away, hurt. That's the difference."

"I'm not serious about Noah. If I have to not be upset at him to prove that, then fine, I'm no longer upset."

"Right. Just like that."

"Just like that."

"Because you don't do 'getting close.'"

"Right."

Her sister sat there quietly, making her fidget. "Why don't you?" Savannah finally asked.

"You know why I don't."

"If I did, I wouldn't ask."

Katie sighed and looked up at the darkening sky, debating whether she really wanted to get into this now. "It's best to just have a fun time without getting emotions involved. Someone always gets hurt when feelings come into play."

"You sound like a man."

"You're the perfect example of what I'm talking about," Katie said. "You cared. Now look what you're going through."

Savannah's eyes widened. "I'm going through a divorce because I made a mess out of my marriage, Katie. It has nothing to do with caring."

"Come on, Van, don't try to tell me you don't regret the whole relationship. You're in so much pain right now. I hate to see it. Hate that you're hurting so much."

"As much as I've messed up, I do not regret for a minute getting involved with Michael all those years ago. You're completely wrong about that."

"Seriously? Savannah, you're miserable. You wouldn't have that problem if you hadn't fallen in love."

Savannah leaned forward, her eyes burning with feeling. "And I wouldn't have my family. I wouldn't be the same person. This is the craziest thing I've heard from you in a long time."

"Why does not wanting to get hurt make me crazy?"

"No one wants to get hurt, Katie. No one."

"Right. So it makes sense to play it smarter, does it not?"

"Have you never been in love?"

"I've never been in love." Katie rolled the chain of her heart necklace between her fingers and stared back at Savannah, challenging her to prove otherwise.

"No one? You get so much male attention. You really never have been?"

"I don't want to be. Therefore I haven't. Simple as that."

"Methinks the mighty may be falling, Katie."

"Not me." She stood and went inside, dismissing any notion of falling.

CHAPTER NINETEEN

NOAH PICKED UP the patient file from the box outside Exam Room Three and paused when he saw her name on it. He'd known Katie had an appointment today to have her cast removed. Suspecting she was due, he'd pored over the schedule book till he found her listed at eleven o'clock.

He hadn't seen her since she'd left his house, angry, two nights earlier. Yesterday had been a very long Sunday, but he'd fought the urge to chase her down and apologize. When she left town, he'd have to get used to not having her there. He'd told himself all day that this was good practice. A much needed reality check.

Yet he couldn't deny how relieved he was to be able to see her today. Even if she was still spitting nails about their last encounter.

He knocked lightly on the door and pushed it open.

Katie sat on the counter next to the sink. She watched him enter the room and he couldn't read her expression, wasn't sure what to expect from her.

"My favorite patient," he said. "You realize most people sit on the exam table instead of the counter?"

"I'm not most people."

He couldn't detect anger in her voice, but he wasn't about to assume that he was in the clear.

"I owe you an apology," he said, standing far closer to her than he would any other patient. She wasn't his patient right now, not until he said what he had to say in order to make peace. "I'm sorry I was a jerk Saturday evening."

"It's okay. I'm over it."

He examined her face for any sign to the contrary, but found none. Her lips inched into a slow, warm smile.

"Really?"

"Really."

"Because I don't deserve to get off so easily. I was pretty harsh. I'm sorry I said what I did about your dreams."

She shrugged. "No biggie. In fact, it's so not a big deal that I'm calling you on what you promised me."

"Which is?"

"A visit to the river swing, once I'm free of this thing." She held up her arm and flicked the cast.

"You really want to do that? It's not actually all that great."

"I haven't done anything fun like that for five weeks. Trust me, the swing's a start."

He couldn't help feeling as if he was getting off surprisingly easy here, but he wasn't about to question it. "Meet me here after work and we can go swing."

She nodded, satisfied.

"Now are you going to move to the table so I can get that cast off you?"

"I think the counter will work just fine," she said, pulling him closer for a kiss.

KATIE MET NOAH at the office again after his shift. They decided to use the Tahoe and pick up Katie's Jeep later. He drove to the park.

"I thought we were going to the swing," she asked, confused.

"We are. The back way."

She looked at him thoughtfully, waiting for an explanation.

"I don't feel like making small talk with my parents."

"Fair enough." She didn't, either, considering she'd been looking forward to spending time with Noah all day.

They got out of the vehicle and walked down the jogging trail in the opposite direction from their usual route. The trail ended fairly soon and Noah took Katie's hand to lead her down the overgrown dirt path.

"You have to promise me something," he said. "If I let you try the swing, you mustn't support your weight with your left hand yet."

"You said it's healed."

"It is. And I'd like to keep it that way."

"Me, too. My big day at the event-that-shall-not-be-spoken-of is coming up soon."

He turned around and frowned at her, so she blew him a kiss.

They emerged from the underbrush to grounds that had been neatly mowed. Noah's parents' house was visible through the clearing. Katie eyed the swing, tied to the tree once more, and sped toward it, dropping her towel on the way. "I'm first!"

Noah helped her untie the restraining rope and held on to the swing as Katie stripped down to her hot pink bikini.

"How deep is the water out there?" she asked, playing with all kinds of cool ideas.

"Twelve to twenty feet in most places. What are you plotting?"

She climbed onto the swing, careful not to let her left hand support all her weight, just as Noah had advised. "I told you, I'm jumping off."

"I'm not sure that's a good idea."

"It's deep enough."

"What if you hit the dock?"

"The dock is twenty feet away."

"What if you get tangled up in the rope?"

"What if the tree gives out and falls on me?" she retorted. "Noah, relax!"

"I'm not watching."

She rolled her eyes and pushed off with her feet, leaning back to increase her speed. The sensation of flying made her let out a happy yell. She'd been earthbound for far too long.

"Have you ever gone double?" she asked as the swing lost momentum in his direction and began its descent back over the water.

"I am not getting on that thing with you."

"Killjoy!"

He sat down and leaned against the tree the swing was suspended from and Katie could see his eyes were closed. Was he seriously afraid of a rope swing?

She whooped again and Noah's eyes popped open. He was not smiling, either.

Katie arched her back and pumped her legs forward. This time when she was coasting back out toward the middle of the river, she released her grip and flew into the water. She yelled as she hit the surface, laughing at the simple thrill of it as she went under.

She surfaced, still smiling and then she looked over at Noah. His expression was serious. In fact, Katie saw him sag back against the tree as if he'd actually been afraid she might not come up at all.

Katie climbed out of the water using the old ladder at the end of the dock. She picked up her towel and wrapped it around her waist before sitting down next to him. "Your turn."

If she'd thought ignoring his weird behavior would resolve the problem, she'd thought wrong.

"Not today." He wouldn't even look at her.

As she studied Noah's face, she saw sweat dotting his forehead. Then he rubbed the back of his neck, as if he'd hurt himself.

"What's wrong?" she asked.

He took a deep, slow breath and she

wondered if he was simply going to ignore her.

"Noah?"

He gazed out at the river, but she'd bet he wasn't really seeing it. Something was going through his mind, and it wasn't the notion that it was a good day for fishing.

"It terrifies me watching you do things like that," he said.

"Noah, I'm safe. I'm okay." She rested a hand on his leg. "It's just a river swing. You used to do it all the time yourself. Why are you acting so weird about it?"

He shook his head, seeming to have things he needed to say but unable to say them.

"Are you okay? It's not that hot out here. Why are you sweating like that?"

"This isn't just 'normal' worry. I seem to have developed a fear of physical danger, especially when it involves those I care about."

Katie frowned. He wasn't supposed to care about her. Not like that. Not beyond a temporary friendly affection.

"I know very well my fears are mostly irrational, but that doesn't seem to change anything. Images pop into my mind of worst-case scenarios. Lots of them. Anytime I think about you putting yourself in danger, I just about lose it. My head throbs, my neck becomes so tense I can barely move it and sometimes I break out in a sweat."

"Did that happen just now, when I was on the swing?"

Noah nodded.

"Noah, look at me. I'm *okay*." She tried to control her instinctive annoyance.

"I don't expect you to understand."

Except he did, of course, or he wouldn't have told her about it.

"Have you talked to a shrink about this?"

"I'm a doctor. I've read up on it. But I can't seem to make it go away."

"You can't let fear run your life, Noah. The best way to deal with it is to face it. Head-on." She certainly wasn't an expert on post-traumatic stress, but she did know what she'd been doing for practically all her life.

"I'm not sure how to do that. Or if I want to."

She stood and stepped back a bit from him, crossing her arms. "You know, when my mom died I was scared to death. Of ever feeling that way again, of depending on someone and losing her, of...lots of things."

"So what did you do at the wise old age of thirteen?" Noah asked.

"Started climbing on the roof and taming wild river rapids."

"I feel sorry for your dad."

Her smile disappeared. "Oh, he handles it pretty well."

"Not from what I've seen."

Katie stared at him. "What have you seen?"

"You scare your dad, Katie. He worries like crazy about you. Maybe even irrationally, like I do."

"How would you know?" Katie refused

to believe Noah had any idea what he was talking about.

"I saw it in his eyes when you were up on the roof that day. I know what it feels like—the sheer terror that something's going to happen to someone you care about."

"He's never said anything to me. I mean, he worries. I know that. All dads worry about their kids." She couldn't help the defensiveness in her tone of voice.

"He worries a lot more than you think he does."

Katie gritted her teeth. "So everything's all because of me. Is that what you're saying? You worry. My dad worries. None of that would happen if I just quit my job and worked for the Lone Oak newspaper. Right?"

"I'm not saying it's your fault, no. Not entirely."

She bit down on the things she wanted to say because none of them were very nice. But she didn't want all these problems laid on her. She was who she was.

And being involved in anything more than a fleeting, passing-the-time relationship was not a part of her.

"So what are you going to do?" she asked. "Just wait till crazy Katie's out of your life and see if the extreme anxiety goes away?"

"I wish I believed that would happen." He shook his head.

"Face the fear," she said adamantly, her frustration seeping through. "Hiding from it doesn't do any good."

Facing it had always been her way. It was how she did what she did. She embraced the challenge of whatever activity she needed or wanted to do. After a while, the rush of fear became addicting, because she knew that soon after she'd experience the high of overcoming it. There was no other feeling like it in the world.

"Forget I said anything," he said. "It's my problem."

Katie frowned as she pulled her shorts back on over her suit, wishing she *could* forget. Wishing she could leave without the least bit of concern for Noah. Wishing that she didn't care.

"I'm sorry I don't know how to help you, Noah, other than walking away from everything I do that scares you. I guess the lucky thing is that I'm leaving town in a few days."

"Let's just try to pretend I never brought it up and enjoy the time we have left."

She knew that wasn't entirely possible, but she'd always been a believer in denial. She could still try to play that game for her last few days in town.

She picked up her T and drew it over her head.

"Are you going somewhere?" he asked.

"I need to talk to my dad."

Noah stood and held out his hand to her. They walked back to the parking lot without talking any more and she tried to ignore the tension emanating from Noah. When he dropped her off at her Jeep, she kissed him quickly and told him she'd see him later.

CHAPTER TWENTY

KATIE WENT DIRECTLY to her dad's new house, not caring that her swimsuit had soaked through her clothes or that her hair was a tangled, soggy mess.

When she rang the doorbell, no one answered, but both cars were in the driveway. She headed around the house to check the backyard.

When she got to the quaint wrought-iron gate, she spotted them on the opposite side of the yard by the garden. Her dad sat on a gardening stool, with Claudia kneeling beside him. Katie stopped, taken aback by how old he looked.

Nothing had changed, but perhaps she hadn't really *seen* him for quite some time, hadn't noticed how gray his hair was, how etched the wrinkles in his face had become. From this distance, she could tell his movements weren't as spry as they'd once been.

He bent forward, using a trowel to pat down the dirt around a flowering plant they must have just put into place in the garden. Claudia watched him, waiting for him to finish. She held a watering can at the ready.

When her dad finished his task, he straightened, slowly, stiffly. But he smiled as he watched his wife water the new plant, his eyes crinkling with contentment.

It struck Katie then, how good it had been for him to remarry. She'd always said she wanted him to be happy and she thought she'd meant it, yet all along she'd struggled with this new relationship. Only now did she understand what this new marriage meant and she was truly glad for him.

Claudia finished her watering and then stood. She turned to Katie's dad and took his hand, helping him straighten up. He bent to give her a quick peck on the lips.

Katie actually smiled as she opened the

gate. "That's enough, you two. No making out in the backyard."

Her dad met her eyes warily, as she walked toward them. "You're in a good mood."

Katie didn't correct him. "Time for a drink?"

"We were just going to have a cold lemonade," Claudia said. "Want to join us?"

Katie nodded and walked behind them up the three steps to the deck. "I'll get an extra glass," she said.

When she returned with a glass, her dad and Claudia were sitting quietly, probably wondering what in the world was up with her. She sat at the table and poured herself lemonade.

"What brings you here today?" her dad asked. "We haven't seen much of you since we moved."

"I wanted to ask you something." She took a sip. "Noah tells me he thinks you worry incessantly about me and my job."

Her father stared at her expectantly. "That's not a question."

"Do you?"

He ran his hand over his mouth, obviously thinking about his answer, which told Katie plenty.

"Of course I worry about you, honey. Your job is extremely dangerous."

"Noah says he thinks maybe it goes beyond normal worry. Like it's a losing-sleep kind of worry for you. You don't lose sleep over me, do you, Dad?"

A quick glance at Claudia gave her her answer. Yes. He lost sleep worrying about her.

"Why didn't you ever say anything?" she asked.

"What good would that have done?"

Katie shrugged and leaned on the table. "I just didn't know."

"I'd never ask you to change what you do, Katydid, no matter how much it scares me."

"Um, thanks, I think." She studied his features intently, counted the wrinkles, happily noting that most of them appeared to be laugh lines. "Is there anything I can do to make you worry less? Besides quit?"

"You could start by staying off the roof." He softened his gruff plea with a smile.

Katie looked up at the roof of the new house. "This one doesn't look like nearly as much fun. And besides, there's no good way to get up there."

Katie took another sip of her lemonade, wanting to somehow apologize for the way she'd acted ever since she'd been back in town, but not knowing where to start. "The garden looks great."

"All Claudia's doing. She lets me help sometimes, but she's in charge."

Katie met Claudia's gaze across the table. "You're good for him."

"He's good for me, too," Claudia replied.

Katie gathered her courage, trying not to squirm over the things she had to say. "I need to apologize to both of you."

Her dad watched her steadily and Claudia rested her elbows on the table, leaning closer.

"I've had a hard time with you remarrying, Dad. It's never been anything against you, Claudia, but I'm betting it probably seemed like it was."

"We knew it wasn't easy for you," Claudia replied.

"And selling the house…" She looked at her dad. "I was pretty mean about it."

He took her hand and held it. "Don't say anything else. I know how hard it's been."

"I'm not over losing it yet. Don't get me wrong," Katie told him. "I've just decided to stop taking it out on you." She offered them both a sheepish look. Then she exhaled nervously, stood and hugged her dad. "Love you."

"Love you, too, Katydid. Do me a favor?" She pulled back far enough to look him in the eyes. "Don't you go worrying about me dealing with your stunts. This lady here helps me an awful lot."

"I probably can't change the way I am," Katie said. "I'm sorry it affects you, though."

She walked around to Claudia and gave her a quick hug, as well. "Thanks for taking care of my dad. I'm betting he's a handful."

"And then some." Claudia beamed at her.

"Okay, no offense, but I've had enough touchy-feeling emotion stuff for one day. I'm gonna take off now."

"Going to see Noah?" her dad asked, and she stopped in her tracks.

"No. I don't think he really wants to see me right now."

"I'd be mighty surprised if you were right about that," her dad said.

Katie decided to ignore him, not wanting to think about her feelings for Noah or his for her. She'd already done far too much thinking and talking today.

"YOU'VE BEEN CRANKY all day," Savannah said to Katie as they prepared a double batch of lasagna. "What gives?"

Katie had decided to leave the following day, instead of waiting for the weekend, and the whole family was coming over for a goodbye dinner. She was antsy, weary of all the emotional strain the past few days had contained.

"I'm not cranky," Katie said. "I just have a lot on my mind."

"Does Noah know you're leaving tomorrow?"

"No."

"Don't you think you should tell him?"

"Don't you have enough to worry about without trying to run my life?"

Savannah stared at her. "You've fallen for him, haven't you?"

Katie glared at her.

"You have. Admit it." Savannah could be so annoying. Such a know-it-all.

"What if I did? What does it matter?" Katie asked.

She'd had an uneasiness in her gut ever since Noah had confided in her about his irrational fears the day before. She'd tried hard to ignore it, to remind herself that she was leaving soon and it didn't matter what she felt. But Savannah had come to the same conclusion she had less than twenty-four hours earlier.

"What does it matter?" Savannah repeated, staring at her in disbelief. "What does it matter? This isn't even worth discussing, if that's what you honestly think."

"That's what I honestly think, so let's drop it."

"Sometimes I want to shake you till the rocks in your head line up in some kind of order." Savannah measured out ricotta.

Katie welcomed the noise of the electric mixer. It was a lot less challenging to deal with than the tangent her sister was currently pushing. Unfortunately, the break was all too short.

"Katie, honey, I don't get it." Savannah faced her again, her hand on her hip. "What's so bad about caring for someone like Noah? He's a good man. What's to dislike?"

"What's to dislike?" Katie laughed, a bit harshly. "That I can't stop thinking about him. I miss him, and it's only been since this morning that I haven't seen him. I hate that."

"So go see him."

"I don't want to. I don't want to care about him. I can't."

Savannah stared at Katie. "I get that you don't want to be hurt. You don't want to lose anyone else. Mom's death messed you up and you don't want to go through that kind of loss again. I understand that. But…"

"There can't be any buts."

"*But* you've already fallen hard, Katie. The damage is done. Give it up and go to him."

"My life is somewhere else. Doing something he can't accept."

"Your precious career. Yeah, yeah. I know. It's easier for you to dangle over a canyon thumbing your nose at mortality than it is to open up to someone and let yourself care." Savannah turned back to the counter again and lined up lasagna noodles at the bottom of a casserole dish, then poured a layer of meat sauce on top.

"It's not thumbing my nose at mortality, it's conquering my fears."

"Conquering your fears. Interesting."

Savannah pursed her lips thoughtfully. "Wouldn't it be even more interesting if you stopped focusing so hard on conquering your fear of physical danger and instead tried to conquer your fear of emotional danger?"

"What on earth does that mean? Emotional danger. Are you studying to be a shrink on the sly?"

"If I were, I'd charge you big bucks for this invaluable advice. You know, you and Noah are exactly the same. It's almost funny."

"Hilarious, I'm sure. Why am I sitting here listening to Ms. Lonelyhearts preach to me about my faults?"

Hurt flickered in Savannah's eyes and Katie immediately regretted her words, no matter how angry she was.

"Oh, Van. I'm sorry. That was low."

"Yeah. Whatever. I know I'm not in a great position to be handing out advice just now, but this one is a no-brainer."

"Yeah. Go back to work, back to my life," Katie said. "You can't really expect me to give up my career for him, can you? I don't even know how he really feels about me, other than that he's freaked out by some of the things I do."

"That's a pretty good indication of how he feels." Savannah stopped working and faced Katie, lasagna apparently forgotten. Who could focus on cooking when there was a lost soul to set straight? "You're scared of losing someone. Noah's scared of the same thing. You've both lost big time and, believe me, I understand that."

Katie wished now she hadn't told Savannah about Noah's past.

"His solution is to bury himself in a safe, little town and hide from everything," her sister continued. "Yours is to run around the country on one big adventure after another and avoid personal commitment. You two are more alike than you think."

The part about Noah struck Katie as similar to something she'd said to him herself. She tended to agree—Noah had decided he would be safe from emotional harm here in Lone Oak.

"I'm not avoiding anything. Why does everyone assume that just because I have a wild job I love I must be hiding from something?"

"Maybe it's obvious to everyone else, Katie."

Katie shook her head adamantly. If she found herself on her deathbed tomorrow, she wouldn't be saddled with a laundry list of regrets.

Would she?

No. She'd *lived,* even in her relationship with Noah. She'd enjoyed every moment. Just because it wasn't going to be a long-term relationship didn't mean she was losing out.

A faint question niggled at her, deep inside, but she didn't have it in her to consider it more closely.

"Isn't this where you run away in anger?"

"As a matter of fact, you're stuck with

me. I'm hungry and I have nowhere better to go."

So what if she was avoiding Noah only because she'd figured out how she really felt.

CHAPTER TWENTY-ONE

NOAH FOUGHT DRIFTING off to sleep as he
tried to catch up on a medical journal. He
glanced at his watch—it was after ten. He
doubted Katie was coming over.

But just as he formed the thought, he
heard knocking at the back door and his
heart began to beat faster. It could only be
her at this hour. Jumping off the couch, he
headed for the back door.

He opened the door, not bothering to
turn on the overhead light. Katie wasn't
smiling. He pulled her inside and kissed
her, relieved beyond describing when she
responded.

"I thought you might not come over
tonight," he said, still holding on to her,
thrilling in the feel of her in his arms. He
would never have enough of this.

"I wasn't going to." She stiffened and

backed away. "I'm leaving tomorrow, Noah."

"Why so soon?"

"It's just…time for me to go."

Deep sadness constricted his chest, even though he'd known this was coming. What difference should four days make? Of course, until now, he'd done what she'd suggested and put her departure out of his mind. No more denying it.

The sense of loss hit him hard. Instinctively, he needed to fight it, to avoid losing another person he loved.

Another person he loved.

There was no question about it, although he hadn't had the thought before this moment. He loved Katie and he didn't want to lose her. Watching her walk away now would likely be at least as horrible as it had been to lose Leah.

"Come, sit down," he said, taking her hand and leading her toward the living room. "Let's talk."

"It's not going to change anything."

Desperation pulsed through him. What could he do to make her stay?

He sat on the couch and gestured to her to sit in his lap. Surprisingly, she took him up on it. Noah put his arms around her, wanting never to let her go.

"Katie, stay with me."

"I have to go back. I start work on Monday."

"We could have a few more days together."

She absently played with his hair. "What good would that do, Noah?"

"I don't know. It'd give us some time together. To have fun. That's what this was supposed to be about, right?" He wasn't willing to just give up. He had to lay it all out for her now, be honest with her, even if it didn't do any good in the end.

"It's not very much fun with a goodbye hanging over us. I'm not sure how that happened."

He swallowed, his throat tightening. "Katie, we both went into this knowing it would end. I had no intention of anything but enjoying your company and having someone to help me paint." He smiled briefly and she flicked his chest.

Noah ran his finger over her heart-shaped locket. "But something happened that I wasn't expecting. The thing is...I love you, Katie. I don't want to lose you."

Katie felt her eyes fill with moisture and her head threatened to explode with pent-up emotion. This was so painful. This was *exactly* why she never wanted to fall in love. She looked into Noah's eyes, barely seeing him through the blur of tears. "I love you, too," she whispered, putting her arms around his neck and burying her face in his shoulder. "But sometimes love isn't enough." They held each other for several minutes, and Katie fought off a crying jag the whole time.

Finally, Noah eased his embrace enough to have a look at her. She hated the tears that still stood sentinel in the corners of her eyes.

"Stay here with me, Katie. Move back to Lone Oak."

"I can't do that. You know that."

"If we want it enough, we can make it work somehow."

"You're asking me to quit my job. Give up everything."

His gaze fell and for one instant Katie tried to imagine what it could be like if she agreed to his request. She shook her head.

"What if you quit your job for now? Gave me some time to get used to your risk-taking? Maybe you could go back to it later."

"There's no 'getting used to it,' Noah. You told me the other day you don't know if you can ever get over your fear. You don't want to try hard enough."

He didn't say anything, which told her she was right. "Why should I give up everything, when you'd still get to keep your safe little life here? Where's the compromise in that?" Her voice broke, but she continued to speak. "What you're asking is so unfair."

"I know," he said in nearly a whisper. "It's not going to happen. I don't think I'd truly want it to, even as much as I want you here. The last thing I want to do is ruin your life."

But that didn't make her feel better at all, because it still came down to the same thing. They loved each other, and yet there was no way they could be together. Neither one of them could give the other what they needed.

"You have to love all of me, Noah. And that includes the crazy parts just as much as the injured-and-can't-do-anything part. That's who I am."

"I know." His voice was husky, heavy with sorrow.

Finally her tears spilled over, and she couldn't stop a sob from escaping. Noah pulled her close again and she cried against his shoulder. This was so ridiculous. They were trying to comfort each other over the pain they caused each other. If she didn't feel so miserable, she would've laughed at the absurdity. Instead, she burrowed in deeper and held on for dear life.

"Stay for a while, Katie. We don't have to say goodbye just yet."

She straightened, shaking her head. "I can't. I have to go now." She bowed her head again. "I'm sorry. It's too hard."

The thought of prolonging it even for a few more hours made her shudder. It was time to make a clean break. Holding on any longer would do neither of them any good.

Katie walked slowly toward the front door, and Noah followed.

"You can call me anytime," he said.

Katie shook her head, unable to speak, her throat was so swollen with the pain of leaving.

"You're right," he whispered. "It'd just make it harder."

Katie coughed nervously, switching gears, mostly out of self-preservation. "I need my medical forms faxed so I can go back to work. Can you handle that?"

He nodded. "Yeah. I'll take care of it tomorrow."

"I have to leave now. I can't take it." Her temples throbbed as she turned away.

"Goodbye, Katie." He spoke the words she'd tried to avoid as she went out the door.

If she looked back she knew she would lose it completely.

CHAPTER TWENTY-TWO

NOAH SAT IN his crummy rental car staring at a map. This had to be it—the trail leading to the area where Katie was supposed to make her climb.

He grabbed his backpack, got out and went over to a large wooden display board that held a more detailed map than the one he'd been studying, as well as posted information on the trails and the climbing area. Granger Cliffs, it was called. The man back in Boulder, who'd given him the map and explained how to get here, had told him it was a tough but popular climb.

Apparently the climb itself began about three-quarters of a mile up the trail. Noah sucked in a lungful of crisp mountain air, trying to bolster his courage, and started along the path to the cliffs.

It had taken a lot of nerve to get him this far.

The week after Katie left, he'd been in the worst possible kind of misery. In addition to the huge void in his life where Katie had been, there was the self-loathing. The anger at his own failure. His weakness.

He'd spent five whole days being impossible to be around, beating himself up, just...mad.

Day six finally had given him the idea that it was time to do something about his fear, the irrational thing that had seemed to take on a life of its own and was keeping him from a future with the woman he loved.

Tracking down information about Katie's big climb, the one she'd been so excited about, the one he'd shut her down about every time she brought it up, hadn't been too difficult. Being buddies with her dad had helped.

The other break was the medical seminar in Denver that was taking place at the same time. He was legitimately interested in the seminar topic, but it had taken an outside motive to make him sign up. A last-minute booking allowed him to participate and kept the real purpose of his trip obscured. Noah hadn't been able to tell anyone about the personal stakes involved in this trip. He worried that once he got there, he'd flip out and not make any progress toward facing the fear of Katie's extreme career. She didn't know he was coming, either.

The path forked, causing Noah to consult a sign. He followed the one to the right and finally managed to pull himself out of his thoughts sufficiently to take in his surroundings.

Aspens and pines towered over him on both sides of the path. Mountain peaks jutted up above the treetops. Birds and squirrels flitted about along the path. A cool wind whipped through the leaves, offering striking relief from the heat of the big city. He wondered if it might be too windy for a rock climb. Surely they wouldn't allow

Katie to attempt it if the danger was too great.

All too soon, he became aware of people up ahead—voices, a backpack propped against a boulder. He slowed nearly to a stop, taking in the scene.

The clearing appeared to be the spot where the ascent began. Twenty or so people milled around, some with cameras and others with climbing equipment. Apparently, the wind wasn't a problem for these people, although it certainly made him uneasy. More uneasy.

Noah stayed back among the trees and pulled his baseball cap a little lower. He chose a large rock to sit on. He could see the base of the cliff from there, but anyone would have to be looking hard to notice him.

His heart pounded for a multitude of reasons. Anticipation of seeing Katie after two and a half weeks was a huge part of it. He scanned everyone there, but he didn't immediately spot her. Then…he craned his head to see around a tall, skinny man who was watching someone intently.

Katie.

He knew it was her just from the way she stood, hand on a hip, one long, gorgeous leg perched on a rock in front of her. He could read her enthusiasm in her body language from all the way back here.

The skinny guy stepped to the side, allowing Noah a better view. He was more determined than ever to overcome his fear. He needed this woman in his life. He hadn't exactly worked out the details of how that might be achieved, didn't even know what being here today to watch her would accomplish. All he knew was that he was afraid to be here and afraid not to be.

If he could get through this, however, and somehow eventually accept the part of Katie that was so much the heart of her, then perhaps they could figure out the rest.

Noah moved to a rock that afforded him a better view. She was so intent on what she was doing, he doubted she realized how many people were around her at all. From what he could tell, she was conferring with an instructor who was explaining everything to her. She nodded frequently, as the man held up different pieces of equipment.

Noah knew she wasn't a novice climber. Even though they'd avoided the topic most of the time, she'd explained to him that she climbed at an indoor gym for fun. Even so, she was clearly taking in every word of advice the instructor had to offer.

The skinny guy motioned to one of the men who were laden with camera equipment, directing him to take several shots of Katie and the instructor.

Noah was fascinated, watching it all, and became temporarily distracted from the fact that in a few minutes Katie would risk her life by climbing—he glanced up— an extremely sheer rock face. In heavy wind.

The tension at the back of his neck flared and he felt sweat appear on his forehead. He took several slow, measured breaths. He was going to get through this without succumbing to black panic.

As soon as he'd confirmed the arrangements for this trip, Noah had contacted a psychiatrist friend of his back on the east coast. He'd briefly explained his problem and had gratefully noted several internet sites the doctor recommended that dealt with overcoming fears. Now it was time to put his crash course to the test.

When he looked for Katie again, she'd moved closer to the base of the rock. She now wore a harness of some sort, which gave Noah only token comfort. He knew little about the sport of rock climbing, so he wasn't sure of the different pieces of equipment and how they worked. Reaching into his pack, he took out the binoculars he'd bought at a sporting goods store in Boulder.

He noticed that four or five of the people, Katie included, had stopped their preparations and were now gathered in a group, seeming to discuss something—heatedly. The instructor dug out a cell phone and made a call. When he hung up, they had another discussion. Noah wished he were close enough to hear what they were saying.

When they took positions close to the rock again, Noah held the binoculars, trying not to draw undue attention to himself. He looked through them, aching to see Katie's face. Of course, her back was to him. Her honey-brown hair was pulled into a knot on the back of her head, out of her face. As he was about to lower the glasses, her feet caught his attention.

Those shoes. He'd seen them before. When she'd been waltzing around on her dad's roof.

He'd thought they were strange-looking tennis shoes at the time, but he hadn't given them much consideration since he'd been otherwise engaged with not plummeting to his death—or watching Katie drop over the edge.

She'd been wearing rock-climbing shoes on the roof. They gave her better grip and traction, he'd bet.

He lowered the binoculars, thinking about this.

Leaning back against the rock, his mind spun.

While he'd assumed Katie had been throwing caution completely to the wind, she had obviously taken the time to put on shoes that made her stroll on the roof safer.

Again, the group discussed some issue, but this time Katie did most of the talking. She shook her head several times, gestured to the rock above, and he could tell she felt strongly about whatever it was she was saying.

The instructor nodded once, said something, and the group broke up. They removed the equipment they'd already put on and each one headed to his pack. Katie took a bottle of water from her own bag and sat down next to the instructor, talking much more calmly now.

Noah noticed one of the guys from the group stalking his way on the trail. He made eye contact with him. "What's going on with the climb?"

"The chick called it off. She wants to wait out the wind. Thinks it's too dangerous right now," the guy explained.

Noah glanced back at the others to double-check that Katie was the only "chick." "You don't agree?"

The guy shrugged. "I'm just ready to get up the mountain. Been waiting for this for a long time."

Noah nodded, as if he understood, and the climber continued down the path.

Katie was the levelheaded one who had the sense to wait for the wind to die down? The guy who'd walked away thought *he'd* been looking forward to the climb, but Noah had seen with his own eyes how excited Katie had been when she'd first learned of the assignment.

Between her shoes and her decision to wait out the wind, Noah was perplexed. Stunned, really.

All this time, he'd imagined she was just like Leah. Now, it hit him like a lead weight that they were actually quite different from each other.

Leah had been impulsive to an extreme, often failing to think through decisions and acting only on gut feeling or emotion. Katie was just as spontaneous as Leah, it seemed, but she approached decisions, last-minute or not, with a sense of level-headedness that might have saved Leah's life.

From what he'd seen today, Katie took safety very seriously and triple-checked herself at every step.

Another of the group made his way down the trail and Noah decided it was time for him to leave. He had to be back at the seminar for the final session, anyway. He'd promised his dad he wouldn't miss a presentation being made by one of his old med school buddies. Besides, he still wasn't ready for Katie to see him here. There was a lot to process.

He put the binoculars away quickly and headed back down the path toward his car, thinking back to other instances with Katie in Lone Oak. When she'd plotted her plunge from the tree swing into the river, she'd first asked about water depth and had calculated the distance to the dock and the shore. It had escaped his notice at the time because all he could think about was the rising panic in his chest.

Even when she'd skated into his office to have him resew her stitches on that very first day, she'd been covered with safety equipment from her head to her knees.

Why hadn't he thought about this before?

Because he hadn't wanted to, he admitted. His knee-jerk reaction had been to consider her out of control and dangerous.

Actually witnessing her taking part in something dangerous was still going to be a challenge for him. He didn't expect the miracle of escaping a strong physical reaction, but just figuring out that Katie wasn't actually out to tempt death was going to help a lot. He found he didn't dread watching her so much anymore, just because of this new understanding.

He realized for the first time that he

could trust her to be careful. To take care of herself.

That trust just might make all the difference in the world.

"WELCOME BACK TO LIVING," Katie said to herself as she got in position to start her ascent. The wind had finally died down enough so that it was safe for them to climb. She knew at least one of the others thought she had been too cautious, but they'd only had to wait an hour and a half. And now the climb would be much more enjoyable, less of a battle. Safer.

Today was the day she'd been waiting for ever since she'd gotten the assignment. She couldn't believe her good fortune to get paid to go rock climbing. This was also her reentry into the part of her job she loved most. She'd been counting down to this moment for weeks.

So where was the usual heart-in-her-throat thrill that came before one of her adventures? Why wasn't she feeling it yet?

It was gorgeous here. Acres of trees, dramatic rock outcroppings, a cornflower-blue sky that went on forever. She'd always loved this part of Colorado, loved the feeling that she was a tiny, insignificant part of such a big, beautiful landscape. Loved the earthy combination of pine and fresh air.

For some reason, though, she was having trouble getting back into it.

Today, she couldn't quite get the full force of the feeling. Something was… missing.

Maybe she just needed time to readjust, get her adventure feet under her again, pull her mind away from Lone Oak.

She shrugged and concentrated on listening to the instructor as he continued to explain what they were about to do in great detail. This was the toughest climb she'd ever attempted, and she couldn't afford to miss anything he said.

Right before they began the actual climb, Katie did something she'd never before allowed herself to do. She let in the what-ifs.

What if she messed up? What if her rope

broke or her equipment failed? What if she or her partner did something wrong and got hurt or…died? What would that do to her family? How would her dad handle that, after he'd finally stopped mourning the wife he'd lost and found happiness again?

What would Noah say?

Probably something akin to "I told you so," except she wouldn't be around to hear it.

She pursed her lips and closed her eyes to focus. This was stupid. She thrived on risk. Now wasn't the time to freak out about all the possibilities. That only weakened her.

She wasn't going to mess up. The guy next to her would see to that, just as he'd seen to her equipment, checking and double-checking that it was all in perfect condition.

At the instructor's signal, Katie held her breath and began the slow trip upward. It took her exactly two seconds to get herself completely into the moment.

Thank goodness, she thought briefly. *Everything's going to be okay.*

CHAPTER TWENTY-THREE

BUT EVERYTHING WASN'T OKAY.

Katie packed up the equipment that belonged to her after the climb, feeling empty and more than a little concerned.

What was wrong with her?

The only thing that had gone well today was the climb itself. She'd been out of sorts and had let her mind wander too much beforehand. And now that it was over, where was that sense of accomplishment that usually made her feel lighter than air?

Normally after an "eyewitness," she was on top of the world, invincible. Today, she was just...mellow. And couldn't wait to get back to her hotel room.

She and the others from *Rush*—a photographer and her editor—piled into their rented SUV to make the drive back to their hotel. Derek, the photographer, was driving. Katie sat in the backseat and kept to herself.

"Salinger, what's wrong with you?" Derek asked. They'd worked together plenty and usually got along well. "That was an amazing climb. Usually you won't shut up afterward."

She shrugged. "Guess I'm tired today. I think I'll take a nap when we get back."

He glanced at her in the rearview mirror, his forehead creased with concern, so Katie threw him a smile. Anything to get him to leave her alone.

At the hotel, she made a beeline for her room. Once there, she stretched out on the hard bed, but it turned out she wasn't sleepy. She was restless, out of sorts.

She sprung to her feet and looked around. For what, she didn't know—she was wondering what on earth was going on with her.

Her usual routine after an exciting day was to come back and have a drink with any colleagues who'd traveled with her, grab some dinner and hang out with them.

Derek was one of her favorites, but she'd just as soon watch paint dry as be social with him—or anyone else—this evening.

She looked out the hotel-room window and saw a fast-food place just across the street. Grabbing her purse and throwing on some shoes, she set off for something to eat, hoping that would snap her out of her mood.

Waiting in line at the restaurant, she grew impatient. She wanted to go home. Immediately. This hotel, this city, this hamburger joint… None of it was doing a thing for her.

She made a snap decision and felt a small amount of relief.

Katie opened the oversize purse she used when she traveled and dug out her airline confirmation form and left the restaurant without bothering to get any food. She punched in the airline's number on her cell phone as she headed back across the street. Finally, an attendant answered and asked if he could help her.

"Yes. I'd like to move my flight up from tomorrow morning to tonight."

KATIE HAD SPENT THE FLIGHT back to St. Louis deep in thought, mostly about Noah. Why she was thinking about him now, she couldn't say. Of course, he'd been on her mind almost nonstop since she'd driven out of Lone Oak, but she would've thought that today, of all days, she could push him aside and focus on the job that meant everything to her.

She paused, the key to her apartment in her hand.

The job that *used* to mean everything to her.

It hit her now, suddenly, as she let herself in, that something else meant more.

Someone else.

Unfortunately, there wasn't a thing she could do about it. She could quit her job and move back to Lone Oak. But that would only solve half the problems between her and Noah. It would still mean he couldn't accept a very important part of her life—a very important part of *her*.

Katie went to the freezer and pulled out a half-eaten pint of Ben & Jerry's. She grabbed a spoon, then sank down onto the couch, feeling despair in a way she'd never felt it before.

Not only was it impossible for her to be with the man she loved, she was discontented with the career that had previously defined her.

What she wouldn't give to be with her family right now, back in Savannah's kitchen arguing over lasagna or letting off steam with her niece and nephews at the playground. She missed her dad, even Claudia. And she would kill for a home-cooked meal.

She dug out the last spoonful of ice cream and found she was still unsettled and completely unsatisfied.

Maybe she just needed to sleep on everything, see how her life looked tomorrow. Because right now, it all seemed about as wrong as it could get.

She couldn't convince herself to get up and unpack or even flop down on her own bed. Instead, she flipped off the lamp and stretched out on the couch, fighting back tears. She should be exhausted enough after the climb, the trip home and the emotions that plagued her to drift off to sleep without a problem. Key word being *should*.

She still hadn't moved forty-five minutes later, except to turn over several hundred times trying to get comfortable, when someone knocked on the door.

Katie sat straight up, thinking she'd heard wrong, since it was well after midnight. No one would visit her this late.

She sat stock-still, listening. A few seconds later, she heard a knock again, a little louder than before. She crept to the door and looked out the peephole. Her heart jumped up into her throat when she saw the outline and blur of a man with Noah's build and hair color. Forgetting caution, she unlocked the door.

"Hello, Katie," he said, the familiarity of his low, smooth voice warming her to her toes.

She stood back so he could come in, but she didn't know what to say. So many thoughts were racing through her mind, she couldn't keep up. Her apartment was still dark, the only light coming from the outer hallway, but she didn't even notice. She shut the door and locked it out of habit.

"Did you forget to pay the electric bill?" She could hear the humor in his voice, and when the question finally registered, she felt her way to the lamp by the couch and turned it on. And feasted her eyes on him.

His hair was messy, clothes wrinkled, eyes tired…but they also had a bright spark of happiness in them.

"What are you doing here?" she asked.

"Just flew in from Denver." He looked at her as if that should set off some kind of realization, but it didn't. Other than registering that she'd just come back from there, as well.

"I did, too," she said, which made him smile. Knowingly. "Noah? What's going on?"

"I saw you there, at the cliffs."

"Granger Cliffs? You did?" She sat on the couch, curling her legs under her, trying to absorb the implications. "What... Why? How?"

Noah chuckled. "That medical seminar I told you about? The one in Denver? I ended up signing up for it."

"Ohh," she said, trying to understand, but not quite there yet.

Noah sat down on the coffee table right in front of her. "I've missed you so much, Katie."

Her heart threatened to pound right out of her chest.

"I was lost when you left," he continued quietly. "How that happened so fast, I don't understand, but it did. It took me several days, but I finally figured out that I had to do something about the fear that was running my life. Ruining our chances together."

He rested his elbows on his thighs and took both of her hands in his. Katie stared at their intertwined fingers, unable to sort through her thoughts enough to say any-thing.

"Long story short, I used the seminar as an excuse to show up at your rock climb this morning."

"You were there? I didn't see you."

"I didn't want you to see me."

"Why not?"

"Because what if I went all that way and then still freaked out, as you would say, when you started up the side of the mountain?"

"But you didn't?"

"I didn't have the chance to, when you called off the climb."

"Postponed. We went up an hour and a half later."

Noah was smiling widely, shaking his head. "It didn't matter. Because I finally figured out something."

"Like what? That I'm fabulous and I've been right and you've been wrong all along?"

He laughed. "Actually, that's pretty close to the truth. I need to apologize for the way I've misjudged you." All signs of joking disappeared from his face. "I made the mistake of thinking you were just like Leah—wild and irresponsible—from the very first time I met you."

Katie tried to stop the smile that was tugging at the corners of her mouth. "I may have egged you on a bit in that direction."

"A bit?"

She pinched her index finger and thumb together. "Tiny bit."

He grabbed her fingers and kissed them.

"In all seriousness, you scared the day-lights out of me, Katie. But today, I finally understood. You're not the same as Leah. You may be half crazy, but at least you do it in a responsible way." He looked earnestly into her eyes and Katie melted. "I've figured out you don't want to die, that you do everything you can to protect yourself from harm. Like the shoes on the roof..."

Katie's eyes widened. "My climbing shoes?"

"I had no earthly idea those were climbing shoes until I saw you in them today."

She lost herself in howls of laughter, falling back on the couch, closing her eyes and chortling from deep in her belly like she hadn't done for years. "You thought I was prancing around up there with no extra traction?"

He didn't answer, or if he did, she missed it because she was still laughing so hard. When she could finally breathe again, she straightened. "I knew I was messing with you but I thought it was obvious that those shoes helped me not to slip and slide off the edge."

"No. I didn't know."

She snickered again. "So you figured that out today."

He nodded.

"And if I'd just explained to you that I wasn't as nuts as you thought I was and that I was actually pretty careful up on that roof, would we have alleviated all the awfulness of the past few weeks?"

He was pensive for several seconds. "No. I still needed to put it all together."

She became serious. "So are you telling me that you can handle my career now?"

He sucked in air slowly. "I don't know that I'm worry-free, doubt I'll ever be. But what I can tell you is that I trust you, Katie. I understand you don't want to get hurt any more than I want you to get hurt. I'd like to watch you on a few events, try to work through the panic. I'm ready to try that now. Because frankly, panicking about your antics is still far better than not having you in my life."

Katie threw herself forward and wrapped her arms around Noah, then pulled him off the table and onto the couch with her. She drew his lips to hers and kissed him to make up for every day they'd been apart. "I love you," she said when they finally stopped to breathe. "I've been so messed up in the head, but the one thing I know is I want to make it work with us."

"Me, too. I'm not sure how to do that yet, being in different cities, but we can work it out."

"You know," she said, everything falling into place at last. "I may be as crazy as you thought, because suddenly, quitting my job doesn't seem like a problem."

"You can't do that. It's too important to you."

She put a finger on his lips to silence him. "This job specifically?" She shook her head. "I think, if I talk to my boss, I could probably continue to work as a freelancer with *Rush*. And I have other contacts in the industry, too. A travel magazine with an extreme travel column—they've approached me before. If I freelance, I can work from anywhere in the world."

"Including a small, peaceful town in northern Kansas?"

"Especially a small, peaceful town in northern Kansas."

"Katie, are you sure that would make you happy? Is that what you want?"

She didn't hesitate, nodding. "I've missed my family since I left. Lone Oak wormed its way into my heart over the past couple of months. But mostly there's just this overserious, worrywart doctor I can't seem to live without."

"To think you told me there was nothing for you in that little town." He held her close and kissed her slowly, full of tenderness. "I love you, crazy Katie."

Her heart felt as if it would float right out of her body as she hugged him tight.

"So..." she said in his ear. "Where do we go from here?"

"Well, I happen to have this big house. It's a bit oversize for a bachelor. It definitely needs to be filled up with a family. I think you just might like it."

She laughed. "I think I just might, too. So when would this house-sharing thing start?"

"As soon as possible. Let's get married right away. What do you say?"

She ran her fingers through his thick hair and stared into his no-longer-weary green eyes. "I'd say that sounds like the biggest and best adventure ever."

* * * * *